# wherever
# nina
# lies

Also by Lynn Weingarten

*Bad Girls with Perfect Faces*
*Suicide Notes from Beautiful Girls*
*The Book of Love*
*The Secret Sisterhood of Heartbreakers*

# *wherever*
# *nina*
# *lies*

LYNN WEINGARTEN

POINT

ISBN 978-1-338-29178-0

10 9 8 7 6 5 4 3 2 1     18 19 20 21 22

Printed in the U.S.A.      23
This edition first printing 2018

Interior illustrations by Vicky Newman
Book design by Yaffa Jaskoll

*To sisters*

# ONE

The guy walking toward me is good-looking in a jerk way, like he'd be on a reality show about dudes who won't stop cheating on their girlfriends, or a spokesperson for a line of energy drinks. He has on these big mirrored aviators and a tight black T-shirt with *I CAN BENCH PRESS YOU AND YOUR BENCH PRESS* printed in red on the front.

"Hi," I say. "What can I get for you?" I've been working here for a year but I still find it funny when I hear myself ask that, like I'm a kid playing "coffee shop," instead of a sixteen-year-old who actually works at one.

"Give me a sugar-free skim iced chai," he says. "Large."

"A sugar-free skim iced chai," I say. And I try not to look over at Brad, who I can feel watching us through the glass pastry case he's washing.

"Hey, Ellie!" Brad calls out. He's using his best "casual" voice, which is about twice as loud as his regular one. "Isn't this such a *coincidence*? How we were just talking about sugar-free skim *iced chais* and how much you love them? And now this customer is ordering a *chai*? What was that funny thing you were saying about them? About sugar-free skim iced *chais*?"

The thing that's fun about Brad is that he'll say pretty much anything to anyone; this is also the thing that makes me want to lob a muffin at his head sometimes, one of those scary-huge ones that we sell here for $6.25.

I turn back to the guy and shrug, like, "Who is this wackadoo?" But the guy is staring at his phone, swiping and swiping the pictures on his screen.

I make his drink and hand it to him. He watches the muscles in his forearm as he pays, starts walking toward the door, then marches back and slams his drink on the counter.

"No way this is skim," he says. He jiggles the cup. "You gave me a different kind of milk, didn't you?"

He takes off his sunglasses and gives me a piercing stare, as though now I'll be forced to fess up.

"I promise I didn't," I say. "That was definitely skim."

"You're positive about that?" He holds the cup up above his head and looks at the bottom of it, as if that's where all the fat has deposited itself.

"I'm positive," I say. "But I can make you another one if you want."

"No," he says. And then he raises his eyebrows. "But I think we *both* know what you're trying to do here." And then he turns and storms out.

I wait two beats after the door closes, then I turn toward Brad. We burst out laughing. "Wow," Brad says. He stands up, holding the spray bottle and rag. "I thought he looked kinda cute when he first came in, but I should have known his big, shiny glasses were hiding a face fulla weirdo. Never a dull day at the coffee shop!" Brad shakes his head slowly. "Arms like that do not come without a price."

"Um, speaking of weirdos . . . ?"

"Yeah, but *I* was doing it *as a favor*! It is very generous to give two people your weirdness to bond over!" Brad puts the bottle and rag under the counter and glances at the clock. "Okay, Princess Peach, you're off soon, so before you go, I'm going to run to the back and restock real quick. If anyone comes in who I might think was your soul mate, make sure to tell him I said that he should give you his number!"

"Ha-ha," I say.

"I'm serious," Brad says. "Your very own Thomas could be right around the corner."

I roll my eyes. Thomas is Brad's boyfriend who he met while working here. Thomas was a customer and Brad, who never gets nervous around anyone, was so nervous he dropped an entire carrot cake on the floor. And then Thomas was like, *Good job! That's exactly where carrot cake belongs!* And they have been happily in love ever since.

"Truly though, what's the point of working in a coffee shop if you don't get to meet a cute boy because of it?"

"Oh I don't know," I say. "My vast and impressive paycheck?"

"Don't forget your incredible boss!"

"Him, too . . ."

Brad reaches out and boings one of my curls, then flashes me a smile as he disappears into the back room.

I pretend to think it's silly whenever Brad talks about finding me a boyfriend, that I don't even *want* one. But if I'm being honest about it, that's not the case at all. I guess telling yourself you don't have something because you don't want it feels less depressing than wanting something you can't figure out how to have. I'm sixteen and in two months I'll be a junior, and my entire romantic history up until this point consists of three random kisses with three random guys, friends of whomever my best friend Amanda was with at the time. Just once I'd like to kiss someone because we actually like each other, not because we've been left alone by our respective friends, who are hooking up in the next room, and have run out of stuff to say.

I look out over the counter. It's quiet in here, pretty average for an early Friday evening, before the nighttime rush. There are a dozen or so people typing on laptops and reading and chatting quietly. A lanky guy with bright orange hair and an earring in each ear dumps his paper cup into the garbage and turns to wave as he walks out. Earl Grey, double tea bags, with extra milk — that's what he drinks when he comes in here, which is every month or so. Why do I know this? It's the funny thing about working in a coffee shop, I guess, the things you get to know about so many random people, the things you notice.

Two girls approach the counter.

One is younger than I am, maybe fourteen or so. The other looks about eighteen. The younger one has this enormous, bright, ecstatic grin on her face. The light is pouring out of her. When you see a smile this genuine, it makes you realize how many of the smiles you see during an average day aren't.

The older one has the exact same smile. And she has the same eyes. And a similarly shaped face and . . . There's a weird tugging inside my chest as I realize something — they're sisters, these girls. Instantly I know everything about them. And I feel a little sick.

They haven't seen each other in a while. The older one was at college, or away on a long trip, and she's finally returned home. When she was gone, it felt like she'd been gone forever, but now that she's back, it's like she never left. Growing up, they fought a lot. Younger was jealous of Older, resented her and all the stuff she got to do that Younger didn't. Older had always thought Younger was a pain who would never leave her alone. But years have passed since then, and all that petty stuff that once seemed so important stopped mattering, the way it always does. Or the way it's supposed to, anyway. They realized they can be friends now, real friends. And it means so much to both of them because they know how much they went through to get here.

I take a deep breath and try to keep my face expressionless. I know it's not fair, but I suddenly hate them.

"Hi!" says Younger, perky behind long bangs. "We would like, um, some banana bread and . . . LaurLaur?" She looks up. "What else should we get?"

"Um, are the brownies good?" Older asks. And then lightly smacks herself in the forehead. "Why am I even asking, right? They're *brownies*. So yeah, a banana bread, and a brownie of course, and a croissant . . ."

Younger starts giggling. "And another croissant! An almond one!"

5

"And an iced matcha latte," says Older. "And a cupcake and a smoothie and . . ."

The girls keep ordering, exchanging glances, their smiles growing bigger and bigger, like coming here and ordering all this food is the culmination of a private joke, something they'd been discussing for all the months while Older was gone.

I make their drinks and try to avoid eye contact. They're chatty in that way people are when they're giddy with joy, a little high on how happy they are.

"I love this place," says Younger.

"I know, I really missed it," says Older. "Come to think of it, it's probably what I missed most while I was gone. Most of everything and everyone in the world!" She opens her eyes really wide and Younger mock punches her in the arm. Older grabs Younger around the shoulder and kisses her on the cheek and Younger pretends to wipe it off. They both laugh.

I finish lining their food up on the counter.

"Oooh, sorry!" Older says. She pays for everything with crisp new bills. "Thank you so much!" she says.

"Yes! Thank you!" says Younger. "So much!" It's as though they're giving me credit for how happy they are, as though by being there to witness it, I had something to do with it.

It takes them three trips to carry all their food over to the table. Normally, I would have offered to help. But right now I don't. I can't. Older puts money in the tip jar — three dollars. No one ever puts in more than one.

Less than a minute later Brad is back, standing next to me. He watches me watching them, and puts one arm around my shoulder. "It's time for you to go," he says, and hands me a white paper bag. Inside are a dozen broken cookies iced in pink and green and white. "We can't sell these," Brad says. "I was going to give them to Thomas, but you should probably take them instead . . ."

I stick my nose in the bag and take a sweet breath of almondy air. The tightness in my chest begins to loosen. I am, I decide, very lucky to have Brad in my life who, for all his ridiculousness, knows exactly when I might need a big bag of cookie pieces. And also knows exactly when I won't want to talk about why.

# TWO

I'm outside. The air is cooler now and the sun is going down. My eyes adjust to the dimming light as I walk.

I pass a Pilates studio, a design store, a gourmet shop. Mon Coeur, where I work, and Attic, where my best friend Amanda works, are in the middle of Edgebridge, Illinois, which is a suburb of Chicago. It's a fancy place for rich people, the Disneyland version of what a town should be. There are beautiful new streetlights lighting up every corner, and pink and orange flowers blooming in the tall wooden boxes that dot the sidewalk. In the fall this part of town is decorated with pumpkins and ears of dried corn, and in winter it's all glittering Christmas lights and jingle bells. The town is about a two-minute drive from Amanda's house, which is why we both got jobs here in the first place. There's nowhere to work in my neighborhood, except liquor stores and used-car dealerships. Besides, I practically live at her house anyway.

Amanda's waiting for me at the door to Attic. She kisses me on the cheek. Then she stands back so I can see her outfit. "What do you think?"

She's wearing a tiny pair of navy blue running shorts, and a tiny white tank top. She has a pair of navy blue soccer socks pulled up to her knees.

"Are those children's clothes?"

"I got them in the boys' department."

"Well, if you're trying out the prepubescent look, you forgot about a couple of rather important, ahem" — I stare at her boobs — "things."

"Ha-ha," she says. She adjusts her socks. "My parents are out tonight and so I'm thinking we should have some people over to swim and hot-tub, including a lot of extremely swoony dudes who we barely even know. I'm sure *they'll* like my outfit even if you don't." She sticks out her tongue and smiles. I can't help but smile back. Amanda has a good life: Her parents love each other, she has two nice, funny brothers who she gets along with, and a giant house where everything is beautiful and comfortable because someone has put effort into making it so, because they have the luxury of thinking about those things.

"What about Eric?" I ask. Eric is Amanda's not-quite-boyfriend whose not-quite-ness is due to the fact that he continues to date other girls.

"I'm done with that idiot," Amanda says.

"Good," I say.

And we both know this isn't true, but we leave it at that.

"I already picked out some stuff for you too, girly," Amanda says. She grabs my hand and leads me toward the back room, where we always try on clothes. "Good thing Morgette is rich and has a country house, right?" Amanda grins, as though somehow she doesn't realize her own family is pretty rich, too.

Morgette, the owner of Attic, leaves early every Friday in the summer to go to her country house for the weekend, and she gives Amanda the keys to the store so she can lock up. Basically this means that Amanda and I can borrow whatever we want from the store so long as we bring it back by Monday morning.

"The clothes are already used," Amanda explained to me once. "So it's not even like it's wrong to wear them. All we're doing is using them a little bit more."

As I get dressed, I fill Amanda in on everything that happened at Mon Coeur with the regulars and the randoms — Decaf Mocha was there on what seemed to be another online date. Extra Shot Latte and her girlfriend are engaged now. I tell her about the angry guy with the aviators, and the girl with the British accent that I'm almost certain was fake. I don't mention anything about the sisters, though. Amanda's my best friend, but even with her there are limits to what I feel like I can say.

A few minutes later I'm barefoot in front of the mirror wearing a tiny boys' white button-up shirt, a wide gold belt, and a floaty white skirt with gold threads running through it.

Amanda is behind me. "Stop frowning," she says to my reflection. "As usual you look hot spelled with about twelve extra *t*'s."

"Ha-ha," I say. I roll my eyes.

Truth is, no matter how much time I spend staring into the

mirror, I don't really have any idea what I actually look like. Does anyone?

I'm not tall and I'm not short, I have curly hair that reaches to the middle of my back. My skin gets blotchy when I get nervous or embarrassed. I blush a lot. My face is round, and so is my nose. My eyes are brown. I have one dimple. In pictures, my smile always looks crooked. I have no idea what that all adds up to.

Amanda tosses me a pair of gold lace-up sandals that could be part of a costume in a play about ancient Greece.

"Try these," she says.

I sit down and slip off my shoes. There's a cardboard box next to me on the floor with *Sunny Grove Citrus* printed on it in orange and green.

"What's in here?" I poke the box.

"Stuff from Crap Day," Amanda says. "It's this new thing Morgette's been doing. The third Friday of every month she'll buy anything anyone wants to get rid of for two dollars a pound."

"Like old bananas and expired vitamins?"

"Basically. I guess enough people accidentally sell her first editions of old books or pieces of antique silverware that she thinks it's worth it." Amanda shrugs. "But really, who knows. It's not like she needs the money."

I crouch down and start digging through it — a bag of plastic spiders, three unopened jars of nutmeg, a huge glob of dried-up neon Play-Doh, empty mason jars, a half-burned candle. At the bottom is a big book with the hardcover ripped off — *Encyclopedia of Abnormal Psychology*.

"Hey, Amanda," I say. I pick up the book. "Do you think we'll find Eric's picture in here under . . ." Something slips out of the book onto the floor.

It's a rectangular piece of cardboard a little smaller than an index card. I reach out for it. As soon as my skin touches it, my heart is pounding, my mouth drops open, and I feel dizzy, like

I've been spinning and just stopped. The room tilts. Everything around me looks wrong all of a sudden, and I think maybe I'm going to pass out.

I'm vaguely aware of Amanda's voice calling my name, but I can't answer. She sounds far away and unfamiliar. Everything is unfamiliar, except for one thing. The piece of paper in my hand covered in blue vines. I stare at them so hard they begin to swirl, like delicate navy thread snakes on a field of white. And in the center of these vines is a drawing of a girl: big round eyes, round face, round nose, crazy hair curling out in all directions, one dimple, a crooked smile.

*I know this drawing.*

I've seen versions of it since I was little, on the backs of notebooks, on napkins, paper tablecloths, in an entire comic given to me once by someone whom I haven't seen in two years, whom I try not to think about because I have no idea where she is or what she's doing or if she's even still alive, whom I've tried to convince myself to stop thinking about as if that were even possible, whom I've almost completely given up on ever hearing from again, whom part of me still believes will reappear, will send me a sign at some time when I am least expecting it.

And this is the sign, and that time is now.

Because this drawing is of me.

I blink and turn toward Amanda, who is still standing there in her ridiculous outfit.

"Amanda," I whisper, "look . . ." And I hold the paper up to the light. "My sister."

# THREE

For three nights after Nina vanished, I didn't sleep. I just lay in my bed, my head inches from the open window, the thick, humid late June air blowing against my skin like hot breath. Waiting.

When I would hear the sound of a car in the distance, approaching the house, my heart would start pounding so hard I could feel it throughout my entire body, I could feel it in my *teeth*. I would imagine my sister inside this car, and that at any moment I would hear the sounds of her coming home: a car pulling up in front, the inside-of-car noises spilling out when the door opened — laughing and music with a heavy bass — the door slamming shut, the quick *slap, slap* of flip-flops against driveway, the slow creak of the front door opening. And then the almost soundless padding of my sister tiptoeing up the stairs. I would bite my lip and squeeze my hands into fists, hoping, hoping, hoping to hear this. But then the car would pass without slowing down, and I would feel the weight of disappointment, so heavy I'd stop breathing. This happened over and over, a dozen times a night, the high of hope, the crush of losing it. Over and over and over. Exhausting, sure, but never enough to let me sleep.

During those three days, I wandered around in a haze. Time stopped meaning anything, faces blurred together. I forgot words. Sleep deprivation is a drug, but a bad drug no one would ever do on purpose.

Finally, on the fourth night, all that adrenaline was trumped by the wet cement coating my eyelids and filling the inside of my skull. As soon as I lay down, I was sucked through my bed into the center of the earth where my brain finally released the thoughts I could not allow it to have during the day. At first it seemed like I hadn't fallen asleep at all, because my dream started off with me awake in my bed. I got up to use the bathroom, and saw a clump of Nina's hair, the bright ocean blue she'd dyed it a week before she vanished, wet and matted at the bottom of the tub. I felt a flood of relief so huge it almost knocked me over, because this meant Nina was here, had been here all along, and, silly me, I hadn't noticed her. I laughed. And then leaned down, picked up the hair — it was heavy, like wet rope. I held it up, but only then did I notice the ragged chunk of skin clinging to the end of it, like raw meat. And I didn't have to wonder, I knew exactly what this meant.

Then everything went black and I heard only a high-pitched animal scream until I woke up, the sound ringing in my ears, unsure whether it came from inside me or from outside.

# FOUR

Here are the facts, just the facts, everything I know, which is barely anything at all: Two years ago, on the afternoon of June 24, Nina Melissa Wrigley disappeared. She went out in the late afternoon, and then, she just never came back.

When she was gone, she was *gone*. She didn't use email. She wasn't on social media. She'd had cell phones in the past, but kept breaking them and losing them and at a certain point decided not to bother getting another one. "If we were meant to be so connected, we'd have phones already built into our heads, don't you think?" Nina said once with a smirk and a shrug.

All her stuff remained in her room exactly as it always had been — clothes in piles on the floor, tubes of hair dye on the nightstand, sketch pads and drawing pencils and pastels and pots of ink scattered everywhere. There was a graduation gown hanging in her closet — Nina had graduated from high school a week before. She'd turned eighteen two months before that.

Nina was an amazing artist. That might sound like an opinion, but I think it's fair to say it's a fact because no one who saw her drawings ever disagreed. She could draw a photographic reproduction of absolutely anything. But real skill, her skill, wasn't in drawing things that were obviously there, but noticing and capturing things that weren't — the unsettling angle of the sunlight in late winter, the scared expression on a person's face that they weren't aware of making.

Nina turned everything into art. She inked elaborate landscapes onto the soles of her Converse, and covered her tank tops in portraits of the people she saw on the street. Every few weeks she'd dye her hair a different bright crayon color to match whatever was going on in her life at the time. Two weeks before she disappeared she'd decided to dye it blue — "graduation-hat blue," she'd called it. I remember sitting in the kitchen with her, watching from my seat at the table, as she squeezed the dye onto her head, swirling it around like someone squirting ketchup onto a plate of fries. "There's some left," she'd said when she finished. She'd held the bottle up and shook it around. "You want a streak, Belly?" And I'd nodded, thrilled to be included, even though my stomach was already filling with anxiety about what my mother would say when she saw it. Nina chose a chunk behind my left ear and coated it. I remember exactly how the dye felt on my head, cold and heavy. I'd put a paper towel on my shoulder to catch the drips. And then we sat there while the dye did its thing, making jokes and laughing and dancing along with some song she put on. I remember thinking this was a sign that finally, finally, I was old enough for Nina and me to really be friends, not older-sister/younger-sister friends, but real friends who happened to be related and I was so happy. Nina hadn't been home much around then,

17

and when she was it was like she was there and not there at the same time. But I remember thinking that day, as we sat there surrounded by the sweet smell of chemicals, that this was the start of something new, that everything would be different after this. And it was, just not in the ways I'd imagined.

Two weeks later, Nina was gone, a dye-stained towel left in a ball on her floor. I never did show my mother the streak in my hair, or anyone else for that matter. I wore my hair down until it faded away so Nina and I were the only two people who ever saw it.

Here's another thing about my sister: Nina did what she wanted. She wasn't reckless, but she didn't worry about things other people worried about — getting in trouble, getting laughed at, looking stupid. She pool-hopped late at night and cut class and talked to strangers. She was the type of person who, if she saw a guy wearing a big cowboy hat that she liked, would say, "Hey, cowboy! Can I try on your hat?" And he'd probably end up letting her keep it.

When she was sixteen, she started sneaking out at night. She'd go to bed like regular, and then many hours later I'd hear her tiptoeing back up the stairs before the sun came up. What she was off doing, I don't really know. She was never barfing drunk, was at most a little giggly. And when I'd ask her where she'd been, her response would usually be a wink or a grin. Nina was an expert at dodging questions.

For a while our mother tried to stop her from sneaking out, but she was working nights most of the time and so there was not much she could do. Besides, Nina was always, always, always home by morning. Well, except until she wasn't.

I wish this next fact weren't true, but it is and there's nothing I can do about it now: The very last time I ever saw Nina, I yelled at her. She'd been about to eat one of the ice-cream sandwiches I'd asked our mom to get from the store. And I stopped her, shouted about how they were *mine* and if she wasn't going to be around then she wasn't allowed to eat them. It was petty and stupid. I was hurt because she'd hardly been spending any time at home, and I missed her. And she had looked so confused. "Belly, I'll put it back, okay?" she said, quietly and so gently. "I'll just go put it back." For months after she disappeared I would replay this scene over and over in my head, imagining a different version of this story in which I let her eat the ice-cream sandwich, in which I gave her the entire box of them, as though somehow that could have prevented what happened next.

Another unfortunate fact: When Nina first vanished, my mother barely seemed to notice. I guess when you spend all night working at the hospital and have seen some of the things she's seen, your worry bar is set a little higher than most people's. "Your sister's not missing" was all my mother had said. "She's just not here." And any argument on my part, that Nina would never just leave us like that, that Nina would never leave *me* like that, she barely seemed to register. I wanted my mother to be concerned, too, so I didn't have to carry this all on my own. But all I got was my mother's somber exhaustion. And what, I swear, seemed like the tiniest hint of relief. Certain lines in my mother's face seemed to soften, like she'd been clenching her jaw for eighteen years and only now could she finally relax.

I gave up on the idea of my mother doing anything and took matters into my own hands. I printed *Have You Seen My Sister?* signs on Amanda's parents' fancy color printer, and Amanda and I hung them up all over town. I called as many of her friends whose names I could remember. I even called our father (who left us when I was seven), who I had not spoken to in over two years. The connection was bad and I had to yell my name three times before he understood who I was. Finally, I called the police. But when they arrived at our house, my mother sent me out of the room. She talked with them in hushed tones in the kitchen over glasses of weak iced tea she'd made from a mix. They left about twenty minutes later seeming unconcerned, while my mother rinsed their glasses out in the sink.

But then the phone calls came. First a few, and then a flood of them, all at once. I don't know if they were from one person or from many because my mother instructed me to stop answering the phone. I remember one night, it was very late and I was supposed to be in bed and the phone rang — it had been ringing all day. I went to my mother's room and saw her through the slightly open door. She was sitting on her bed in her bathrobe. I could only see her back. "Nina's not home," my mother was saying into the phone. Her voice sounded funny, like she was talking underwater.

"No." Pause. "No, I haven't." Pause. "I don't know." Pause. "Nina's not the kind of girl who informs her mother of her whereabouts." Pause. "So stop calling here."

Then she hung up. And she sat there for the longest time after that, receiver cradled in her lap, head hanging down, shoulders shaking as she wiped her face over and over with her hands, barely making any sound at all.

# FIVE

Sitting on the floor of Attic, I'm trying to remain completely still, which somehow feels necessary and important, although I'm not sure why. Maybe it's because I know how fragile things can be, and if I move, I'm afraid I'll pop the bubble of this moment and it will turn out that I've imagined the entire thing. I will look down and the doodles will be someone else's doodles, or gone entirely. I've had this happen before . . . thought something meant something when really it meant nothing at all. But I have waited too long for this to let go so easily.

I don't know how much time passes before Amanda says, "El?" And I look up.

There are so many questions bouncing around inside my head, each trying to get turned into words first. But I make myself take a breath, as much as part of me wants to GO GO GO, part of me needs to slow this down, to hold on to this for a second longer, because right now whatever's going to happen next hasn't happened yet, and moments of thinking *maybe* are so much better than stretches of knowing *no*. But I can't wait any longer so I take another breath and say, "Now what?"

I'm not even sure who I'm asking.

I look back down at Nina's drawing, at my own face. And then I flip the card over. The opposite side has been printed like a credit card — *Bank of the USA* at the top in blue letters next to a little blue and white symbol, *Your Name Goes Here* in a typewriter font under a fake card number at the bottom. I flip the card back again.

And then I gasp because all of a sudden, for the first time since my sister disappeared two years ago, *I know exactly what I'm supposed to do next.* Swirled in with the leaves and vines next to my face is a phone number. *303-555-6271.* I know it must have been there all along and I just didn't notice it before, but part of me feels like I willed it into existence by wanting it so badly.

I grab the phone off Morgette's desk, and somehow I manage to dial.

It starts to ring.

Someone picks up. First there's loud music, a guitar, heavy drums, and a second later, "*He*llo." It's a guy. Southern maybe.

"Hi." My heart is pounding.

"Hey there."

"Hello." I'm frozen.

"Hello again." He sounds amused.

"Do you know a girl named Nina Wrigley?" The words tumble out fast. This is the first time in a long time that I've said her name out loud.

There's a pause. "What's that now?" Someone has turned the music down in the background.

"Nina Wrigley."

He doesn't say anything. I close my eyes. "Do you know her?" I hold my breath.

"Am I supposed to?"

"She wrote your number down on a piece of paper, maybe a long time ago. So you at least met her at some point. "

"Sorry, sugar." He snorts a laugh. "If I remembered every girl who has my number, I wouldn't have enough room left in my brain to remember to wipe my ass."

My heart begins its slow descent toward the floor. "People don't usually forget her, though. She's about five foot six, always had her hair dyed crazy colors, she was an incredible artist . . ."

"I told you I don't know her." His tone is less friendly now. He pauses again. "Deb put you up to this, didn't she?"

"No," I say. "Who's Deb?"

"Yeah, right." He curses under his breath. "Listen, sugar, I don't know any *Ninas* and I never gave my phone number to any girls, okay? So you can go tell your little buddy that she should leave me the hell alone. Tell her I broke up with her for a reason and if she and all her friends don't quit calling me, I'm going to get a restraining order . . ." He stops talking and I hear a woman's voice in the background, "Who are you on the phone with?!" And then a quick whispered, "I swear I'll do it," and then he hangs up.

Amanda has crouched down next to me on the floor. "What happened?"

I have to turn away because I don't want to cry right now. I shake my head. After two years of this you'd think I would be used to it — the thrill of getting to hope, the black pit of knowing there is no point in hoping. Maybe this is just not something people are designed to get used to.

Amanda nods and puts her arm around me, because she's seen me through this kind of thing before, because she's been here with me for all of it. Because she is the closest thing I have to a sister now.

I let my head rest against her shoulder, and breathe in the fancy scent of her fancy hair.

"Oh, El," Amanda says. And we sit there like this for a moment and then I start lacing up those silly gold sandals because I'm not sure what else to do. I crisscross the gold straps around my ankles and try to focus on the fact that the shoes are actually kind of pretty. And it's nice to have a nice pair of shoes on and that is all I'm going to think about right now. I turn to Amanda and force a smile, stick my feet out, and shake them around.

"Well, I'm ready for that toga party now, I guess . . ."

Amanda smiles back, and I can tell she's relieved that I'm trying, that I'm not letting myself sink into that familiar pit. But then before she can say anything, I realize something. And I almost let out a laugh because it is so obvious. I get up and run.

"Seeing my day like this is really kind of an eye-opener," Amanda says, shaking her head. It's a few minutes later, and we're upstairs, watching the Attic surveillance video on fast-forward. "Because I kinda thought I did some work here during the day sometimes, but as it turns out . . ."

I nod, even though I'm not really listening. All my attention is focused on the little people zipping around on the screen: There's Amanda putting on lip-gloss, there's Amanda trying on scarves, there are three girls going through the clothes racks, there's a guy around our age popping a zit in the mirror when he thinks no one is looking, there's Amanda experimenting with different hairstyles.

"It's kind of hypnotizing," Amanda says, shaking her head. "I'm gonna get into wearing braids more often, I think."

A few people come to the counter with bags of stuff to sell, but so far no big white box. No big white box containing the book that contains the drawing that might somehow lead me to Nina. A tall man in a suit appears carrying a box. *Is that it?!* I hold my breath. But he sets it down near the door, tries on a belt, goes to the counter with the belt, discusses the belt with Morgette, picks up his box, and leaves.

Amanda puts her hand on my shoulder. "El, I'm not trying to be a bitch here, and you know that I will do anything that I can to help you, but what exactly do you think watching this is going to do? Even if we do see someone dropping off the right box, you're going to track him down how exactly? Because unless he has his name and address stamped on the top of his head, it's going to be . . ."

But I tune her out completely then because *there he is.*

Stop. Rewind. Play. He's a few years older than us, wearing skinny jeans and a white T-shirt, pale blond hair, skinny arms covered in tattoos, holding a big white cardboard box and walking up to the counter. I watch as he hands the box to Morgette, she takes it to the scale, weighs it, comes back to the counter, hands him some money. He starts heading toward the door, right past where Amanda is trying on hats, but then turns back and . . . this is the perfect part — he goes over to this community bulletin board, takes a red flyer out of his pocket, and pins it up. And then he's gone.

I run back down the stairs, out into the main room, and stop in front of the bulletin board. Amanda is at my side.

"Ellie?" Her voice sounds strained. She puts her hand on my arm and when I turn toward her she's looking at me with such concern that for a second I think she's maybe about to cry. "We don't have any idea how her drawing got into that book, or when she drew it, or how the guy who brought the book here even got it, I mean he could have bought it at a garage sale or found it on the street or . . ." She stops herself and shakes her head. But I don't let it hurt me. I know why Amanda is saying this. I know why she doesn't want me to get my hopes up.

When Nina first vanished, finding her was literally the only thing I thought about. I followed every "clue," certain I was *this close* to finding her . . . like when I saw a girl jogging, wearing the shirt of a band Nina liked, and spent half an hour trying to catch up with her, in case they had known each other. (They hadn't.) Or the time I found a crumpled-up ad for an art supply store in the pocket of an old pair of Nina's jeans and took a three-hour bus ride to get to this store, but they'd gone out of business a year prior. For

27

each of these occasions and the dozens like it, Amanda was always right there with me, as supportive as a best friend could be. And each time when the "clues" led nowhere, I was newly crushed as though Nina had just vanished all over again, and Amanda helped put me back together. As time went on, the possibility that one of these mazes might actually lead to my sister seemed smaller and smaller. And I guess eventually Amanda decided that helping me follow these clues wasn't actually helping me at all.

So I know what she's trying to say and why, but I'm also not going to listen.

I turn back to the bulletin board. I feel my mouth spreading into a smile.

"Ellie . . ."

I take the flyer off the board. I'm not sinking anymore. I'm floating up, up, up, because *here it is.* Bright red paper covered in bold black letters. And I know nothing in the past has worked out, but I also know this time is different. I've been waiting too long for it not to be.

*YOU HAVE HEREBY BEEN CORDIALLY INVITED TO A*
*HOUSEWRECKING PARTY*
*AT THE MOTHERSHIP (349 Belmont Ave)*
*Come help us tear this sucker down.*

*For 15 years we've been home to a rotating band of*
*musicians, artists, transients, travelers, angels, devils,*
*do-gooders, and ne'er-do-wells.*

But we've lost our lease, an era is ending,
the time has come to say goodbye.
Bring your hammers, your crowbars, your spray paint, and
your cameras,
because after tonight
your pictures and your memories will be all that's left.
Friday, June 27th, from dusk til dust.

# SIX

We hear the party long before we see it. The *boom boom boom* of the music, the hum of hundreds of human voices blended together, a loud crash and then louder cheers.

We're near the top of a giant hill, Amanda and I. It's lined on either side by a thick forest, trees curling over the road, threatening to topple over on the dozens of parked cars. We're only ten miles from Amanda's house, but it feels like an entirely different world out here. The houses are huge and far apart, and they all look ancient but perfectly preserved, like this place exists outside of regular time.

"Are you sure that this is a good idea?" Amanda asks.

"There'll be lots of cute dudes there, I bet!" I say. I sound so pathetically earnest, trying to convince Amanda there are plenty of good reasons for us to be here. There's only one I care about.

"Just please, please, please, please," she says. "Please don't get your hopes up, okay?"

I shrug and I give her this small half smile and she shakes her head because we both know it's already way too late.

To our left, two girls are getting out of a dented green car. One of them has bleached white hair and is sipping from a Poland Spring bottle filled with something purple. She's wearing silver lamé boy shorts and a silver bikini top. Swirling silver dragon wings rise up out of her back and point toward the sky.

The other girl is leaning over, looking for something in the backseat, her face obscured by her black braids. She's wearing a black rubber dress, a pair of fishnets, and giant black boots.

"Come on, Freshie," says the white-haired one. Her voice is clear and sweet. It's easy to imagine what she would sound like singing. "My psychic powers are telling me your boyf is this close to hooking up with some other girl. If you don't hurry up, you're going to find someone else attached to the end of his tongue."

"Well, use your psychic powers to tell him he can attach his tongue to whatever he wants!" Freshie laughs. "His tongue is his business. And my business is . . . THIS!" She stands up, a sledgehammer clutched in her right hand, its wooden handle as thick as her arm. "Let's go smash stuff!"

"Wait!" The white-haired one fishes her phone out of her boot. "Excuse me, ladies!" She's talking to us. "Would you mind taking a picture of me and Freshie?"

I take her phone. They put their arms around each other.

Right before the flash goes off, Freshie sticks out her tongue and licks the other girl's cheek. They both burst out laughing. They're exactly the type of people Nina would have been friends with.

I give the white-haired girl back her phone. Then I take the photo out of my pocket, the one I always carry with me. It's a Polaroid of Nina that I found in her room shortly after she disappeared. It might be my favorite picture of her. I don't know who took it, but the way she's looking into the camera, her green eyes twinkling, her enormous dazzling smile taking over half her face, it's as though she's sharing a joke with whoever's behind it. Sometimes when I look at the picture, I pretend that person is me.

I hold it out.

"Have you seen this girl before? Maybe at another party here or something?" Freshie takes the picture from my hand. Her friend leans over her shoulder. They stare at it. I'm not breathing.

"Sorry," Freshie says, shaking her head. "Never seen her."

Her friend shrugs. "Yeah, sorry," and then, "She's cute though!" And then Freshie slams the car door shut with her hip and the girls walk hand in hand down the hill.

We follow them silently.

"Hey," I say quietly. Amanda looks over at me. I can see her eyes shining in the almost-dark.

"Thanks for coming."

She nods and links her arm through mine, and we head down toward the sounds, the party getting louder with every step.

Up ahead is an enormous, eerily beautiful mansion out of another era, but spilling out onto the front lawn is a futuristic art carnival on mushrooms, dressed up for Halloween. There are so many people in every direction I barely know where to look. In the middle of the front lawn is a giant guy with a shaved head, standing behind a giant folding table, wearing an enormous set of headphones. The table in front of him is covered in laptops, turntables, electronic boxes, all the wires leading to a black van that's parked behind him. On top of the van is a row of a dozen giant speakers facing in every direction, blasting opera music backed by heavy electronic beats.

Off to one side a few dozen people are dancing under a massive silver net, dressed up as an assortment of sea creatures — mermaids, mermen, and giant glittering starfish. Up ahead a girl on stilts walks by wearing a flowing dark green wig, holding a long clear plastic tube that leads into a metallic green backpack. She stops in front of a guy who's dressed as an astronaut and holds the tube up over him. He tips his head back and opens his mouth to catch a gulp of gold-flecked drink.

And about twenty feet straight back two shirtless guys emerge from the front door with a green velvet couch hoisted up on their shoulders on which two girls are sitting dressed in jewels and elaborate ball gowns. The guys lower the couch down in the middle of the grass and the girls step off, like princesses exiting a carriage.

For a moment, Amanda and I just stand there. "I guess it's now or never," I say. And we head toward the door as the girls in the ball gowns rev up a pair of chainsaws and start chipping away at the front of the house.

There's a boom, a crash, loud cheers, and then all around me, tiny bits of plaster flutter to the floor like snow. The flakes are everywhere, on my skin and in my hair. When I breathe, I can taste them.

The last three hours have been a series of small disappointments. Since we got here I've shown exactly sixty-four different people the photograph of Nina. And twenty-one of them said she was pretty and nineteen of them liked her hair, but sixty-three of the sixty-four people told me they had never seen her before. And the sixty-fourth couldn't answer because he was busy puking on his shoes.

So now here I am, leaning against the wall in a long hallway, taking a break, just a little break before I dive back into it. Because I'm not giving up yet, I still need to find the guy from the video at Attic. That's why I'm here.

Amanda is outside on the phone (with Eric; she thinks I don't know). I'm alone.

The crowd parts, joins together, parts again, and I realize someone is watching me from across the hallway. Staring, actually. He's tall, six feet maybe, wearing jeans and a black T-shirt. He's totally generic-looking except there's something strange about his face. When I look closer I realize that's not his face at all, but a rubber mask made to look human, with plastic swooped-back hair. The only parts of his actual face I can see are his eyes. Each time the crowd parts, they are locked on mine.

To my left, a girl all in pink is speaking what sounds like pig Latin to a girl dressed as a pig. To my right, a guy all in yellow says to three friends: "Except with more synth and eighties backbeats!" And everyone busts out laughing.

The crowd parts again and this time the guy with the mask is walking right toward me.

"Finally!" he says. "You're here."

Up close his eyes are the color of wet slate. They don't look

34

familiar, and I don't think I recognize his voice, either. "Do I know you?"

He shakes his head. "Well . . . no. But you are here, aren't you?"

"I guess so," I say.

"Either that or you're a very realistic hologram." His eyes crinkle in the corners. "So should we tell each other how we ended up in this crazy place? I mean other than fate of course."

I stare at him. If he's hitting on me — *is he hitting on me?* — at least he's not boring.

"Okay," he says. "I'll go first. So picture it, it's this morning: The sun was shining and the birds were singing slash screaming in existential despair and I was at the gas station and was wandering around in the little mini-mart, trying to procure an iced-coffee drink for me and a gift for you, of course, but didn't see anything you'd like. So I paid for my coffee and I went back outside and what do you know! Someone had stuck a flyer for this party on the windshield of my car. And I'd heard about this place, and had always kind of wanted to see it, but had never been here before tonight. But then I figured it would be my very last chance so . . . here I am! Clearly I was right in deciding to come, although now that I'm here talking to you I'm really wishing I'd gotten you that enormous heart eyes emoji beach ball." I can hear him smiling again. "I'm sorry. I promise I'll get it for you next time."

"Don't worry about it," I say. I feel myself grinning.

"Are you going to tell me your story?"

"Okay," I say. "It was a few hours ago and I'd just left Mon Coeur, which is this coffee shop I work at. And my best friend works at this store called Attic which is right down the street and I was visiting her there and . . ." I pause. On instinct I start fishing for the photograph in my pocket. But then I stop myself as I realize something — if this guy has never been to the Mothership before, that means he couldn't have met Nina here and therefore I don't have to show him Nina's picture and explain that she's gone. And with this thought I feel the tiniest hint of relief. I'm exhausted from telling this story all night, and the truth is, I guess I'm glad to be talking to someone who doesn't need to hear it. And now I'm pretty sure that he's flirting with me. And even though his face is ninety percent obscured by painted rubber, I have to admit I'm enjoying it.

"And we saw a flyer for the party up on the bulletin board. And so we said well why not and now we're here."

"And what about your placement at this wall in particular?"

"I'm just resting for a minute. Actually I'm supposed to be looking for someone."

"Are you playing hide-and-seek?" He tips his head to the side. He's trying to be cute.

"If you are, maybe I could offer you a few tips. You're never going to win standing around like this . . ." He reaches out and takes my hand as though he's going to shake it, but instead of shaking it, he holds it, so gently. Like my hand is very precious and he doesn't want to break it, but also doesn't want to let it go. His hand is strong and warm, the heat of it stretches all the way up my arm.

"I'm Sean," he says. He starts shaking my hand then, as if that's what he intended all along.

"I'm Ellie," I say.

"Well, Ellie, I'm sorry to brag here, but you're talking to a former hide-and-seek gold medal winner and . . ."

But before either of us has a chance to say anything else, a guy walks out of a room off the hallway, kicking plaster chunks with a pair of black boots. His wiry arms are covered in ugly bright-yellow tattoos, and his blond hair is so light you can see the pink of his scalp through it. I breathe in sharply. It's him, the guy from Attic. The guy I'm looking for. He is heading toward the stairs. I push through the crowd after him.

I hear Sean calling after me. "Ellie!" But I don't turn around.

"Hey!" I shout. But the guy doesn't hear me. He's making his way down the stairs. "Stop!" I reach through the railing and I grab his shoulder. I can feel his bones through his shirt.

He turns. His eyes are bloodshot and his skin is pale, blue-veined like blue cheese.

"Iwanted to askyoua questionbecause you soldabunchof stuff toAttic today." The words come out in a jumble. His eyebrow twitches but he doesn't say anything. "I was wondering if I could ask you where you got it?" A couple of people push past us to get down the stairs, a guy and a girl. "The stuff you sold, I mean." The guy whispers something and the girl grabs him by the neck and pulls his face to hers. They're right behind us, their fingers tangled in each other's hair, lips mashing against each other, breathing heavily.

"I do not know what you're talking about," Blue Cheese says finally. A girl walks by wearing nothing but bronze body paint. He stares.

"Attic?" I say. "That vintage store? You brought in a box of items and hung up a sign for this party."

"Why is everyone always accusing me of stuff," he says, and then, "You're mistaking me for someone else, chicky, sorry." He turns and starts to walk off.

"Wait!" I say, a little too loudly. "I kind of know that you did, is the thing. Sell that stuff. It's not like a bad thing or something. My friend works at the store," I add. "All I want to know is where the stuff you brought in came from . . . please?"

Blue Cheese shrugs. His shoulders are tense. He takes a long gulp from his red plastic cup. "I was looking through the basement for stuff to sell, and I found a bunch of old crap. And then I saw that Crap Day sign in the window of that store and I thought, well, what do you know? Why, are *you* in the market for some crap? You didn't have to come all the way here for that, the entire world is full of it!" He lets out a phlegmy laugh, opening his mouth so wide I can see each of his tiny teeth.

"There was one specific thing you brought in, a psychology book and it had something inside of it, a little piece of cardboard stuck between the pages, that someone was using as a bookmark maybe . . ."

From somewhere downstairs the music speeds up.

"And?" Blue Cheese takes another gulp.

"And there were these drawings all over it, and my sister did those drawings."

"So?"

"Well, she's missing," I say. It never gets any easier to hear myself say it.

"And what does that mean?" Blue Cheese's expression changes slightly, the way people's expressions always do when I tell them. His Adam's apple bobs as he swallows.

"It means I don't know where she is and my mom doesn't know where she is." It still feels fresh. It always does. "Two years ago my sister Nina went out and that night she was supposed to come home." He's looking at me like he doesn't know if I'm lying or not. I wish so much, *so much*, that I was. "And she didn't. And then she never came home after that, either."

Blue Cheese is nodding. "Intense," he says. His expression has changed again but I can't understand what the new one means.

"That's why I'm here," I say, "to find you and ask you about this and see if maybe you knew her. I bet she was at this house at some point. Her name's Nina Wrigley —"

"Listen," Blue Cheese holds out his hand, cutting me off. "*Everyone* has been here at some point, okay? That was like the whole thing of this place . . ."

"But I have her picture," I say. My voice comes out thin and desperate. I take her picture out of my pocket and show it to him. He licks his lips and then shakes his head.

"Nope," he says. "Never seen that one."

"Well what about the place where you found the book that her drawing was in? Maybe there's something else there, something else of hers?"

He breathes in and nods, like he's just decided something. He finishes whatever was in his cup and tosses it onto the floor. "Follow me then, I guess." He looks me up and down and then shows me his gums again. "I think I have what you need." And with that my stomach starts fizzling and he grabs my hand. "Come on."

We walk down one flight of stairs. He's crushing my fingers. My brain is overflowing with questions and they bubble out my mouth. "How much more stuff is there? How long has it been there?" But he ignores all of them. He's speeding along now, and I have to jog a little to keep up. We make our way through the living room where a girl is sitting on a swing kicking the wall with a giant pair of platform shoes, through the kitchen where ten people are drinking from a giant fish tank, through a side room where a dozen people are spray painting the walls.

Blue Cheese keeps going and I follow. We go down a long hallway, through a wooden door and down a very, very long flight of stairs in the dark. There's no railing and I'm grateful for his clammy hand now. When we get to the bottom, he reaches up and a second later the basement is illuminated by the faint glow of a single bare bulb. It's bizarrely quiet. The air is cool and damp.

"You could start down here," he says. I look around at the cement walls and exposed pipes. The floor is littered with cigarette butts and old beer cans and empty bottles. There's a sagging beige couch in one corner with a pillow and blanket on it. The blanket is covered in dark spots, mold maybe. But other than that, the basement is basically empty.

I realize he's still holding my hand. He tugs it. "No, down *here*," he says. He glances down at his crotch, and then back up at me. His lips are wet.

He reaches for my other hand and I back away.

"You're lonely. And I get it. But you're not finding what you need because you don't even know what you're really looking for." He puts one hand on my waist. "Maybe I can help you figure it out."

He steps in closer.

"There's nothing else down here," I say. "Is there." But this isn't really a question.

He shrugs. "That stuff I sold to Attic was all there was." And then his face contorts into a bizarrely sweet smile. "Sorry." Then he reaches out and puts his other hand on my ass. I'm overcome with such sadness that at first I don't stop him. I can't even feel it.

But then my brain catches up with my body. And my body floods with adrenaline and I think I'm about to be sick. What am I doing down here? What am I supposed to do now? What the *hell* am I supposed to do now? I close my eyes and I picture my sister, who was never scared of anything or anyone. What would Nina do now?

It's easy as hell to figure out this one.

I bring my knee up as hard as I can between Blue Cheese's legs.

He opens his mouth into an *O* and for a second he is too shocked to make any noise at all. And then his eyes fill up with tears and he starts screaming his head off.

"Thanks for your help," I say calmly. I run up the stairs then and I don't look back.

# SEVEN

I'm back upstairs, part of the party now. I call Amanda. It goes straight to voicemail. Now what?

I walk back the way I came, through the spray paint room, through the kitchen, through the room with the girl on her swing.

I feel someone watching me. For a disgusting second I think maybe Blue Cheese has followed me and I tighten my hands into fists, but when I turn he's not there. I hear the crashing sound of another wall falling. More cheers. I push through the crowd, climb two flights of stairs, and then I'm in a hallway. My eyes burn. It's hard to breathe up here.

Two shirtless guys in painters overalls are coming toward me, each with a giant canvas bag over his shoulder. "Get your hammers here, people, hammers, bowling balls, chunks of scrap metal. Get your hammers!" One of the guys has DEMOLITION CREW written in paint on the front of his overalls. He stops right in front of me. "And for you, sweet pea," he says. He hands me a giant heavy sledgehammer. I tighten my fist around the handle. "No matter what's wrong," he says, "smashing will fix it." He looks me straight in the eye. "It's human nature to want to smash things."

I push my way down the hallway, enter a giant room, and stand in front of a silver wall covered in the black outline of a spaceship. I am numb now, there is nothing in my head but air. I swing the hammer up toward the ceiling, and the weight of it tugs at my shoulder. For a moment the hammer hangs suspended at the top of the arc, and then *whooshes* back down. It connects with the wall and passes right through with a delicate crunch. A cloud of plaster dust swirls away from the new hole. I stare at the ragged edges, the empty space, and I feel a strange sense of relief.

But it only lasts for a second, because then the screaming starts — a girl's voice calling the same thing over and over and over, one word, but I can't make out what it is. And then a flood of people are running past me, one giant writhing unit of arms and legs and heads. A girl trips on her spike heels, and a guy reaches down and pulls her up under one of his arms, dragging her with him, her skinny little legs dangling a few inches above the floor.

And then comes the smoke, heavy and thick, an impossible amount of it all at once. I begin to cough. Inside my head I am screaming, but my whole body is frozen. Hours pass, days pass, years pass, all of time passes in that one second before I hear a voice next to my head shouting, "RUN!"

It's like I've woken up.

"RUN!"

And this time I do.

The air is cotton and I can't even tell which way is out, but I see a girl's back, tumbling forward, and I tumble after her. I take a breath but there's no relief in it. I'm choking, running, my eyes are burning. I hear voices but all I can see is white, everywhere. My arms are out in front of me and the smoke is so thick I can't see my hands. I keep going, keep going, keep going.

Finally I burst out onto the front lawn. The music has stopped. And hundreds of people are outside now. The astronauts, the mermaids, the stilt walkers, the girl in the bronze body paint, a group of guys who look like they're from the future, a bunch of people dressed as robots, Freshie and her friend. They're all out here looking dazed, like no one can quite believe what's happening.

But where the hell is Amanda? Heart pounding, I take out my phone. And then it starts to ring. I answer.

"OH MY GOD, ELLIE!"

She's talking fast, and even though I know I'm outside and that I'm safe now, the panic in her voice scares me. "I was up at the car talking to . . . okay, I was on the phone with Eric, and I smelled the smoke and saw the fire and I ran back down and oh my God!" I tell her where I am. She says she's coming to find me. And then I stand and watch the flames.

A couple minutes later I feel Amanda wrapping her arms around me. We hug tightly. There are sirens in the distance.

"Ellie," Amanda says. "Let's go home."

We walk up the hill, the smell of smoke behind us. By the time we reach the top, the music is back on, mixing with the sound of sirens. I can just imagine everyone back at the party, dancing outside while the house burns all the way to the ground.

# EIGHT

"Princess Peach," Brad says, "saaaaay, *Happy Caturday*!" It's the next day, Saturday, and I am standing behind the counter at Mon Coeur making a latte. I turn toward his phone and raise one eyebrow before he clicks.

"You didn't say it." Brad frowns, then looks at the screen and shakes his head. "Oh dear, this is basically the saddest picture I have ever seen. But through the wonders of my very favorite new app, I can replace your frowning mouth with a variety of famous celebrities' mouths. Including famous animal celebrities and cartoons! Who should we pick?"

I try and smile, but my face refuses. Less than twenty-four hours ago I was on my way to that party. The night was full of possibilities and promise and it had seemed like something magical was going to happen. And I'd felt so sure of it, *so sure of it*.

And now here I am, back at work, as though nothing at all has changed, which makes sense, since it hasn't.

"What's wrong, sweet friend? Tell Braddy and he shall fix it."

If only it were so simple. I would love to talk about it; I am, in fact, dying to. But the thing is, talking about my sister doesn't help. Watching the pity spread over other people's faces only makes me feel worse, makes me feel more lonely. So while one script plays in my head, another one has to come out of my mouth. And it's so tiring, it's all so very tiring.

"Sorry, Braddy," I say. "I . . ."

The bell on the door jingles and then Amanda is walking in, all smiles. "Amanda," Brad says. "Our Ellie seems very sad. How can we help her?"

"I've been trying," Amanda says, and leans over and kisses Brad on the cheek.

"So," Amanda says, turning toward me. "My parents are going out again tonight and I talked to Eric who talked to some random dudes he knows and they definitely want to come over to hot-tub. So, that'll be good, right? We can raid my parents' wine cellar and make sangriiiiiaaaaa!"

I imagine myself in Amanda's backyard, surrounded by people I barely know, unable to get enough out of my own head to say anything at all except perhaps occasionally an awkward ha-ha, so no one asks me what's wrong.

"Will there be any handsome fellows there? Nice dogs or cats? Someone who will help cheer Ellie up?" Brad puts his arm around my shoulder.

"Well . . . Eric has a lot of cute friends," Amanda says. "But I doubt Ellie's going to stop frowning anytime soon."

I feel my jaw clenching. Amanda puts on a slightly different personality when she's around Brad, like she thinks she's going to

46

impress him by acting kind of bitchy. Which makes no sense because he's one of the kindest people we have ever met.

"What's that supposed to mean?" I ask.

"Nothing." Amanda sighs. "Except that I think you're kind of wallowing a little."

"I'm not *wallowing*. I think I have an actual reason to be upset."

"I didn't say you don't."

"The word *wallowing* kinda implies it."

"Well, that's not at all what I meant." Amanda puts her hands on her hips.

"Whatever," I say. My voice comes out sounding meaner than I intended. Regardless of what word Amanda used, I do sort of know what she meant. But I'm frustrated. And I am taking it out on her a little bit.

Amanda sighs. "Look, I think you have plenty of real things to be upset about, up to and including how that loser tried to take advantage of you in the basement last night or how we almost both died in a fire, but . . ."

"Whoa," says Brad. He backs up. "Hold on here. What happened? Are you *okay*, Ellie?"

I turn toward Brad. "I'm fine," I say.

Amanda continues, "I guess I just think instead of thinking about what I know you're thinking about, you should try and take your mind off of it . . . Nothing is really different now than it was yesterday . . ."

"That's the point," I say.

Brad is uncomfortably fiddling with his phone.

"You can't keep doing this to yourself," Amanda says. And then she gives me this look, this horrible look like she feels sorry for me, not sorry *with* me, but *for* me. Like we're totally separate, unconnected people. And I'm all on my own.

"I'm not doing anything to myself," I say. "I didn't choose for things to be like this." My stomach is starting to hurt.

"You didn't. But since there's nothing you can *do* about it, you can choose not to focus on it so much."

I am hit by a wave of loneliness so intense it's like my insides are hollowed out. "No, I can't," I say. I look at Amanda's face, and suddenly she looks like a stranger. "And I thought you would know that."

We stop then. We're all silent.

Amanda's phone buzzes and she takes it out of her giant bag and scrolls through a text chain. "I'm supposed to go meet Liz now so . . . I guess I'm going to go." She drops her phone back in her bag. "Do you still need me to come and pick you up later?"

My cheeks burn. *Need.* That's it, that's the word that gets me. And the way Amanda said it, with the littlest hint of exasperation in her voice, like I'm a chore she has to take care of.

"Nah," I say. "That's alright." I turn around and do something totally unnecessary with the milk jug so Amanda won't see my face.

"Then how are you going to get to my house?" Does she sound confused or relieved?

I shake my head. "I think I want to go home tonight." And a cold heaviness fills the pit of my stomach. I'm not even really sure why I said this, I don't want to go to my house at all. And besides, I think of Amanda's house as home more than I do my own. But it's too late now because Amanda is saying, "Okay then," and, "I guess I'll talk to you later then." And she's kissing Brad on the cheek and walking out the door.

There's a tightening in my chest. I miss Nina all the time, but it is in moments like these, when I feel like I am totally alone in this world, that I miss her the most.

"Ellie?" Brad says again. I just nod, still staring at the door, and then I squeeze my eyes shut and will Nina to materialize. It is dangerous and childish, I know, to let myself wish like this, to pour my whole self into wanting something that I can't have, that I don't even know how to go about trying to get. But I can't stop. I keep my eyes closed and I just stay like that, until Brad tugs on one of my curls.

"I promise I am taking this all very seriously, but my very-cute-boy-who-could-be-Ellie's-next-boyfriend-dar" — Brad motions with his chin toward the door where a guy has just walked in — "is going off! *Beep-beep-beep.*"

I shake my head. I appreciate that Brad is trying to distract me, but I'm not in the mood for this right now.

I watch the guy coming toward the counter with his hands in his pockets. He has a swimmer's body and he walks like a skateboarder, leaning back like he's in no kind of hurry. He's looking at me, like he knows me. Our eyes meet and something inside me flashes.

Brad is squeezing my arm and whispering, *"Beep beep beep."* And as the guy approaches, I feel Brad backing away.

49

He's up at the counter now. He has dark brown hair, which is flopping over his forehead, and a smooth jaw. The corners of his mouth are curling up into a slow, sweet smile. I feel a sudden craving for something, like I'm hungry or thirsty, except not either of those things.

"Hey, Ellie," he says.

I stare back at him. Feel another flash.

"You don't remember me," he says. He blinks. His eyes are the color of wet slate.

This is what his rubber mask was hiding.

"Anyway," Sean says. "I never got to tell you." . . ."

"Tell me what?"

"How to play. Hide-and-seek. Remember? See, you almost got it, but you were missing a key element. Here's how it goes . . ." He grins. "Okay. First you have to close your eyes and count to ten while the people hide. Then you open your eyes and then, and this is really key" — he holds up one finger — "then you *seek* them. See? That's the step you were missing, I think. The seeking one. You had the opening eyes part down perfectly, though, so no need to feel bad." He's nodding, all serious now. "It takes practice."

I wish I weren't blushing. "Well, thanks . . . for the help . . . with that." I am wholly confused by what's going on. But at least I'm not quite as sad anymore.

"Do you want something?" I say slowly. "Like, in exchange for the hide-and-seek lesson? Maybe . . . um . . . a muffin? We sell some very large muffins here. They're not really that great, but they're huge. So if you're into eating a lot of something . . ."

Sean laughs. "No, thanks," he says. "But I'd love an iced coffee if you don't mind. Or you could give me a regular coffee and some ice and I'll mix them together in my mouth."

I go to the big refrigerator to get the iced coffee pitcher. I can see Sean's reflection in the glass, watching me. I pour the coffee, then turn back, and hand him the plastic cup, already covered in beads of sweat. He reaches out to take it. Our fingers brush against each other. An electric shock shoots up my arm. And we just stand there like that, holding the cup together, our fingers touching, until I realize it's time for me to let go.

Brad clears his throat. "Ellie?" he says. He's using his fake voice. He sounds like he's performing in a play. "Since your shift ends in ten minutes, anyway, if you want to head out a little bit early, that's fine with me."

I check the clock on the wall. It's only 3:50. I'm not actually supposed to be done with work until seven. I look at Brad. He nods slowly, his eyes open wide, his lips twitching like he is trying very, very hard not to smile.

"Okaaaaaay," I say, slowly nodding back.

Brad turns toward Sean. "Hey, do you have a car?"

"Yeah." Sean tips his head.

"Great," says Brad. "Can you give your friend Ellie here a ride home? Her ride cancelled on her, and the bus, well, that's just not safe. Besides, it might rain."

My face is burning.

"Sure," Sean says. "I'd be glad to. Hey, good timing on my part, right?" If what Brad said sounds as fake to him as it does to me, he's doing an admirable job pretending not to notice.

"Thank you," I say to Sean. And I'm suddenly very nervous, although I'm not really sure why.

"Bye, El." Brad leans over, kisses me on the cheek, and whispers, "You owe me a latte."

"Ready?" Sean says. Our eyes lock. And there's that flash again.

My stomach twists. "Okay," I say.

# NINE

Outside the clouds are low and dark, and the air is heavy, the way it gets before a storm. Sean leads me over to a navy blue Volvo. "Ta-da!" he says. The paint is scratched and the back bumper is covered in the remnants of bumper stickers that someone tried to tear off, but eventually gave up on — a piece of light blue with a lacy-looking white shape in the corner, a dark green sticker with a white *UR*. He unlocks the door and we both get in.

There are four different plastic cups in the cupholder, and cups scattered all over the floor. On the backseat there's a black leather messenger bag closed with a shiny brass lock. The car smells like pine trees.

"Sorry about all the cups, you can kick them out of the way," Sean says. "Iced coffee is my greatest addiction."

"What a coincidence," I say. "Because I'm addicted to sitting in a pile of cups."

Sean laughs. "I knew there was a reason I liked you," he says. He starts his car. "So where am I taking you?"

"I'm in the Sunrise Village condo complex," I say, "behind the liquor store on Grays Avenue."

Sean drives. Neither of us says anything for a while. I watch his hands as he turns the steering wheel. I cannot recall ever having any sort of opinion about a guy's hands before, but his are beautiful.

"So . . . I have to confess something." Sean reaches up with one of his beautiful hands and pushes his hair out of his face. "I didn't really come here to tell you the rules of hide-and-seek." He pauses. "The truth is, Ellie, it's really not that hard of a game. And besides, you could find the rules online."

"The Internet can be very useful," I say. My heart is starting to race. "But then why are you here?"

"The truth? I looked for you after the party and when I didn't see you I got worried. I thought maybe the fire swallowed you. The fire department said everyone got out okay, but you just never know, I guess." He glances at me and then back at the road. "I remembered you said you worked at the coffee place, so I figured I'd come by and make sure you were alright. I hope that doesn't seem stalk-ery or weird seeing as we only talked for like thirty seconds . . ."

"No, it's nice of you," I say. "I'm okay, thanks for checking."

"You don't look that okay actually . . . When I came in to Mon Coeur, you looked really sad. And at the party, too." Sean pauses. I don't say anything. "So did you ever find him?"

"Who?" I feel myself blushing.

"Whoever you were looking for at the party. Was it that guy with the bad tattoos?"

"Oh," I say. "Yeah. Sort of. I mean I thought so, only it turned out no."

"He isn't like your boyfriend or something, is he?"

"Ha!" I say. "Definitely not."

"Okay, good. I didn't think so. I mean, he didn't seem like the kind of dude I'd imagine you usually date. He seemed kind of like a creep . . . so why were you looking for him?"

I take a deep breath. And I realize I'm going to tell Sean the truth.

"I was looking for my sister," I say. It's not that I've somehow decided this is a good idea or anything, it's just what I'm going to do. "I haven't seen her in over two years." There's no going back now. We're stopped at a stoplight. Sean turns toward me, nodding ever so slightly like, *keep going*. "I didn't think *she'd* be there at the party exactly, I thought . . ." I get the story over with as quickly as I can, spit it out so it's out and I don't have to have the words in my mouth anymore. "I thought if I found the guy who brought in the box, he might know something about where she was, or that someone at the party might." I look over at Sean but he's watching the road again. "But I was wrong." My eyes fill with tears, but I blink them back. "So I guess that's why I looked sad."

"That's a pretty understandable reason," he says.

"My best friend Amanda thinks I need to stop thinking about my sister so much. It's been two years since she disappeared and nothing has changed and there doesn't seem to be anything I can do about it. I don't know, Amanda might be right, it *might* be time to give up." I bite my lip. "But I don't know how to."

Sean is silent. Outside the car, rain is pounding down.

55

"I think I know why I met you now," Sean says finally. He places his hand over mine on the seat between us. "There are some things a person never gets over, that the phrase *get over* doesn't really apply to. And when one of those things happens in your life, it doesn't matter how much time has passed, or if you're sitting alone in your room or at a party surrounded by a hundred people, and it doesn't even matter if you're actually thinking about it or not because no matter where you are or what you're doing, it's still there. It's not just something that happened. It's a part of you."

And then he shuts his mouth and keeps driving. This is it so exactly. And no one else I've ever talked to has ever really gotten it before.

He turns toward me, our eyes meet, and he grins, shrugs, and tips his head to the side, all casual now. "Or, y'know, whatever." And I burst out laughing. It's a real hiccuping, doubled-over laugh, the kind of laugh I haven't had in a long time. The kind of laugh that's very close to crying.

He laughs with me.

"So you get what I'm talking about, then," I say.

"Something like that," Sean says.

"How do you know all of that?" I ask. "I mean, what happened to you?"

But as soon as the words are out, I wish I could take them back. The last thing I want him to think is that I'm mining him for his tragedies, the way I've felt so many others do to me. "Sorry," I say. "You don't need to answer that."

We are pulling into the apartment complex where I live now, the streetlights lighting up the inside of the car. Lighting up Sean's face.

"Seventeen-ten," I say. "Up there on the right." And Sean pulls up in the empty parking spot in front of my front door. "Thanks for the ride." I look out the window, there's so much rain pounding down it's like the whole world is underwater. It's like here, in this car with Sean, is the only safe place left.

"No problem," he says.

I unfasten my seat belt. "So . . ." I know I'm supposed to get out now, but suddenly really, really do not want to. "Well . . . thanks again." I cringe, hearing myself. I start to reach for the door handle and glance over at him one last time.

Sean takes a deep breath.

"I had a brother once," he says. "But he died." There is thunder in the distance. "So that's how I know all this stuff."

I raise my hand up to my mouth. "Oh God. I'm so . . ."

He shakes his head. "It was a long time ago." His face is flushed. "If there was even the slightest chance that I could see him again, that there was something I could do to make that possible, I would never stop trying. Ever." Sean pauses. For a moment we are both silent. "Maybe this is fate, Ellie, me meeting you. Because there's nothing I do that can change the fact that he's gone . . . but maybe what I'm supposed to do now is help you." Sean turns toward me. "Do you think that sounds crazy?"

Something inside me is warming up. I shake my head.

"So should I come in, then?" he says. "Maybe you can show me the drawing?"

I hesitate for only the tiniest shred of a second, enough time for me to look through all that rain at the front windows of our building and remember that my mother is working the night shift tonight, which means she is gone now and won't be home until early in the morning.

"Yeah," I say quietly. "Let's do that."

# TEN

I realize, as we walk into my room, that this is the first time a guy has ever been up here.

I try and imagine how it must look to Sean: messy unmade bed, dresser, nightstand, a desk, a couple of tank tops and pairs of shorts scattered around. It probably seems like no one spends much time in here, which is true since I'm almost always at Amanda's.

I sit on my bed and Sean sits in my desk chair and I continue explaining Nina's drawing. "So then I called the number on there but the guy didn't remember her. And the guy at the Mothership says he found the book in the basement and it was practically empty when I was down there, and even if there were any more clues there, they're all burned up now."

I hand him the drawing and he holds it very gently, turning it in every direction. "This is beautiful," he says. And I know he means the drawing, not me, but still I feel my face getting hot. Then he stops and just stares at it. He doesn't move, he doesn't blink, it doesn't even look like he's breathing. And I'm wondering if he's beginning to regret offering to help me now that he realizes how futile this is.

"No pressure," I say. "I mean, or . . ."

"Ellie!" He says. "I have it!" He flies off the chair and lands next to me on the bed. He flips the drawing over so I can see the fake credit card printed on the back. "This is a cardboard credit card, right?" He taps it with his finger.

I nod, blinking. "Right."

"And do you know where people get these?"

"With credit card offers in the mail, I guess?" I say.

Sean is nodding. "So . . ."

I shake my head slowly. "So . . ."

"So, you said your sister turned eighteen only a couple months before she left, right?"

"Right."

"And credit card companies have access to lists of everyone who's old enough to get a credit card . . . which means chances are your sister probably got some offers in the mail before she disappeared."

"I guess so."

"Well what if she actually applied for one and had one?" He turns the card over and points to the bank's name on the back. "Say from Bank of the USA? If she did, I bet we could sign into her account no problem. All we'll need is her social security number, and then we'll probably have to answer security questions but the answers will all be things like your mom's maiden name and other stuff you'll already know cuz you're her sister."

"Oh," I say. "Okay."

"What's wrong?"

"It's a nice idea! And thanks for thinking of it!"

"You're frowning," he says.

"I don't think it'll work."

"Why not?"

"It's . . ." I pause. My insides are sinking. "I don't know, it's just too easy."

"But that," Sean looks me straight in the eye, his mouth curled into a mischievous little smile, "is exactly why it's going to."

Three minutes later we're in the spare bedroom, which I think of as Nina's room even though my mother uses it for storage and we moved here after Nina was already gone. One of the only times I can remember my mother making a joke in the last few years was right after we moved in. She said, "Ellie, you know you've really made it when you're so rich you have an entire room for only your shoes," and then she opened the door and tossed in a pair of discount black flats that she said pinched her feet but the store wouldn't take back because she'd already worn them. She meant this, of course, ironically. So now this is where we keep all the stuff that has nowhere else to go — old tax returns and report cards and a lamp that was my grandmother's that's too nice to throw out but too depressing to display.

"So apparently I was a super advanced scissor user in first grade," I say, holding up an old report card. I'm crouched down on the floor digging through a big plastic filing box. I still don't think this is going to lead anywhere, but there's no harm in trying. At least it makes me feel like I'm doing something. "But had a bit of a glitter issue." I put the card back and keep searching. Sean is crouched down next to me.

"And you've had all your immunizations," he says, nodding, "which is important." He reaches into the box and pulls out what looks like a small blue notebook. A passport. He opens it.

I look over his shoulder. It's Nina's. In the photo Nina's about the same age that I am now. Her hair is pale pink hanging just above her jawline. She's smiling like she has a secret.

"I guess my mom must have tossed that in there when we moved from our old house," I say. "Nina was already gone then."

Sean is shaking his head slowly, his face is flushed. "You look so much alike it's insane. You could be twins."

"You think?"

I don't believe him, but I'm flattered, anyway.

"You ever think about dyeing your hair like that?" He taps Nina's picture.

"I did a little piece once but that's it," I say.

"It'd look good I bet." Sean shrugs and hands it to me. "You should keep this with you. You never know when you'll need to make a last-minute international getaway."

I laugh, but I do slip it in my pocket. And then look back down into the box I was searching through. A drawing of a little dog is staring up at me, with a curly mustache under his nose and a jaunty beret on top of his head. "Bijoux!" I say. I pick up Nina's drawing. I haven't thought about Bijoux in a very long time.

"What's that?"

"A picture of our old dog," I say. "Bijoux."

Sean is looking over my shoulder. "Was Bijoux French?"

"Yes," I say. "Well, French and also imaginary."

Sean smiles.

"We were never allowed to get an actual dog," I say. "But we got the very best imaginary dog ever." I pause. "Nina got him for us one summer."

And Sean nods as though of course this makes perfect sense. He glances back down at the stack of papers in his hands and then before I can continue he's shouting, "Yes!" and holding out a piece of paper for me to see. "Ellie, look!" It's a photocopy of an insurance claim form. Sean begins to read it out loud. "On October twenty-third, Nina Wrigley had a regular cleaning at the dentist, a check-up, and a set of X-rays . . ." Sean flips the form over and points to a spot right near the top where her social security number is written out neatly in my mother's handwriting. "There it is," he says.

I stand up. "My computer's downstairs."

A minute later Sean and I are sitting side by side on the couch in my living room, waiting for my laptop to boot up.

"Looking at porn on this thing must be a bitch," Sean says.

"Hello, Ellie."

I turn around. My mother is standing in the doorway between the kitchen and the living room, in her bathrobe, drinking juice.

The blood rushes to my cheeks.

She rubs her eyes, half smiles at me. I can't tell if it's because she didn't hear Sean's porn comment, or because she did. My mom is a mystery sometimes. "I haven't seen you in days." She glances at Sean and raises one eyebrow. Sometimes she's not a mystery at all.

"I've been sleeping at Amanda's," I say.

"Oh," she says. "You're sure they don't mind you over there all the time?"

"They don't."

"Okay." She nods, as though we haven't had this conversation dozens of times before.

And then my mom just stands there, not even acknowledging the fact that there is another person beside me on the couch. She's not being intentionally rude, but she doesn't understand things like this sometimes. Like how people act. How people are supposed to act.

Sean stands up finally. "Hi," he says. "I'm Sean."

"Hello," my mother says, awkwardly. "I'm Ellie's mother."

I put my hand in my pocket and touch the drawing. I know I can't show it to her. I wish that I could.

"I thought you were working tonight," I say.

"My schedule changed. I did an overnight last night instead. Got home an hour ago."

"How were the babies?" I ask. I turn toward Sean. "My mom works at the neonatal ICU at the hospital."

"Wow," Sean says. "That must be crazy."

"Preemie twins last night," she says. "Sixteen weeks early. They're stable for now. But it's hard to say what will happen later." My mother shakes her head. There is a special kind of exhaustion my mother always carries around. It radiates off her. When I haven't seen her for a few days, it's all the more obvious. Being around it, I catch it, like a flu. It makes me feel like someone is sitting on my chest. It makes me want to go outside, somewhere light and loud with lots of other people.

"That's awful," I say.

My mom lets out a heavy sigh.

When I was younger I would always beg her to take me to work, imagining all the cute little babies I'd get to play with, but she never said yes. Then one day when I was nine or ten, Nina showed me a picture online of a tiny preemie, born seventeen weeks early. "Mom worked with this baby," Nina told me. His head reminded me of an apricot — small and covered in downy little hairs. His tiny arms and legs as thick as my pointer finger, his skin nearly translucent. According to the article that the picture was attached to, the baby only survived for three hours. Looking at that picture and knowing that filled me with an almost unbearable sadness that I didn't even fully understand at the time. It's like I wasn't only sad for the baby and his family, but for everyone in the entire world. This baby reminded me of something that we are all born knowing, but that if we're lucky, we get to forget: the world doesn't make sense. And things just happen, often without any reason, and life isn't fair, not usually.

I understood my mom in a different way after that.

"I guess I'm going to go back upstairs to nap now," she says. I watch her walk away in her bathrobe, clutching her mug.

"Hey, Mom?" I call out. For a second, one brief second, even though I know better, I consider telling her what's really going on.

"Yeah?" My mom turns back. She looks so tired.

"Sleep well," I say.

And then she's gone.

"Your mom's pretty cool," Sean says. "Didn't even mind that you have some random dude sitting here on the couch?"

"I'm not sure if *cool* is the word I'd use exactly," I say. "But thanks."

"Better than my mom," Sean says. He's smirking. "Who is insane."

I look down. The laptop's finally booted up. Only when I hear the door to my mom's room creak shut upstairs do I start typing.

I do a search and go to the bank's website. It loads slowly, a picture of a man and a woman, sitting at a computer, each with a cup of coffee, smiling.

*Customer log-in* is written on a blue rectangle on the right. And underneath there are small letters in a script font.

*Forgot your username or password?*

I click and am taken to another screen. *Please answer these questions to access your account:*

*Account Holder's Name?* I type in N-I-N-A W-R-I-G-L-E-Y and press return. And then I suck in my breath, my heart pounding as the webpage reloads.

"If she doesn't have an account, it'll tell us, right?" I ask. But Sean doesn't answer.

A new screen has appeared: *Primary Cardholder's Social Security Number?*

"Does this mean she has an account? I think this must, right?" My voice sounds higher than normal, which is what happens when I'm freaking out. Is it possible this could actually work?

"I think so," Sean whispers.

I type in the number.

*Date of birth?* My hands are shaking.

*Please answer the following four security questions.*

"Almost in," Sean whispers.

*Mother's maiden name?*

R-A-I-N-E-R.

*Name of first pet?* When Nina was six, she got a hamster. I was too young to remember, but I remember hearing the story about how my dad took it back to the pet shop because it wouldn't stop squeaking. His name was Squeekers spelled with two *e*'s and no *a* because she didn't know how to spell squeak. I type in S-Q-U-E-E-K-E-R-S.

I hit return again. I feel like I'm about to vomit.

*Name of elementary school?*

E-A-S-T O-R-C-H-A-R-D E-L-E-M-E-N-T-A-R-Y.

The last question pops up.

*Favorite song?*

I start to smile.

"Nina's favorite song was 'Happy Birthday,'" I say.

I type it in. Hit *return*.

The screen goes white and a tiny globe spins in the upper right corner of the screen. I bite my lip. And then a new message appears.

*Welcome, Nina Wrigley.*

"Holy crap," Sean says.

"Oh my God," I say. And I raise my hand to my lips.

I click on billing history archive. There are only two charges. One for $855 at Edge Sports in Edgebridge, Illinois, three weeks before she disappeared. And one for $11.90 at a place called Sweetie's Diner in Pointview, Nebraska, a week after she was gone.

"Nebraska," I say. "What the hell was she doing there?"

"I don't know," he says. And then: "Maybe we should go to the diner and find out."

I turn toward Sean.

Is he serious? He cocks his head toward the door.

I raise my eyebrows.

He grins.

*I think he might actually be serious.*

I bite my lip. Sean is almost a complete stranger. But somehow it's like I already know him. And he really seems to want to help me. And right now he's the only person in my life who does. And I need to find Nina. And this might be my only chance . . .

I look at Sean again. His eyes are open wide, he's nodding ever so slightly.

I take a deep breath.

I nod back.

And that's how it's decided.

# ELEVEN

The summer I was twelve our mother sent Nina and me to stay with our Great-aunt Cynthia at her beach house. She had insisted it would be good for us to have a change of scenery, to get out in the sea air, and spend time with our aunt. "But what she really means," Nina had told me the night before we left as she stuffed her old blue duffel bag with handfuls of tank tops, "is that it will be good for her to have us gone."

"Ugh, I know," I had said, and rolled my eyes like *yuck how annoying*. But secretly, I was thrilled about the trip. I loved my aunt's weird house and the warm Dr Peppers she kept in the pantry and the lemony soap in the bathroom and the fact that her house was so close to the beach that sand blew in under the door and one time we found a little crab walking around the living room like he owned the place. But what I was most excited about was the promise of an entire summer of just me and Nina.

Nina complained a lot leading up to the trip, but everything changed as soon as we boarded the train for our aunt's house. We made our way through the car until we found two empty seats. Nina pushed both our bags up into the racks, and when the ticket taker came by and said, "Tickets please," Nina turned toward me and winked and then said to the ticket taker, in a flawless French accent, "Oh, but ov course, 'ere arr our teeckets."

And after the ticket taker was gone, Nina turned toward me and said, "Oh, I forgot to tell you, Belly, this summer we're French."

I remember the rest of the ride like a hazy dream, leaning back with my knees against the seat in front of me, looking out the window at the power lines and trees whizzing by, feeling like I'd won a fabulous prize in a contest I hadn't even known I'd entered. Without Nina's friends around, I had been promoted to the number one spot. I wasn't just her little sister anymore, I was half of Team Nina, which was about the best thing a person could ever hope to be.

The first four days were perfect. In the mornings we went to the beach, with a bag of books and Nina's little Bluetooth speaker, and lay out on our towels and talked in our accents, discussing the details of our made-up French lives: We were the daughters of French aristocrats and we lived in a French mansion and had a pet dog named Bijoux. Every so often, while we were walking on the beach Nina would randomly call out, "Bijoux? Come here, Bijoux? Where are you, *mon cheri*!?!" as though Bijoux was missing and we were out trying to find him. At some point every day we'd go swimming and at some point after that we'd take a walk on the boardwalk and get lunch and then maybe play Skee-Ball or air hockey, and buy a million snacks from the arcade vending machines for dinner. Our aunt let us do basically whatever we wanted, so long as we stayed together and were home by nine. Every day felt so magical and amazing and unreal in its preciousness. I must have somehow known it couldn't really last.

On the fifth day Nina met Nick. I knew from the second he came up to us, tall and lanky in low-hanging surf shorts, bearing two "lemonade ice-pops," that he was going to ruin the rest of my summer. I wanted to tell him that lemon was our least favorite flavor of pop. And reasonable people like cherry the best and then grape and then orange, in that order. I also wanted to mention that, by the way, when lemonade is made into a pop, you're just supposed to call it a *lemon* pop, you don't need to say the "ade" part. And besides, my sister and I did not need some random doodah to buy us ice-pops anyway because we had our own money and please go away now. But Nina accepted them with a flirty smirk and a coy *merci*. And in that moment something shifted. Up until then the accents were about me and Nina having a joke together. Or at least that's what I'd thought. But watching Nina "ex-Q-zeh mwa see voo play" made me realize it was Nina's joke all along. I had been welcome to participate. But it was always hers and never mine. Most of what my sister did had nothing to do with me.

After that, Nina and I had a new routine: We'd get up, pack our bag, and go to the beach, and then I'd spend the rest of the day all by myself under the umbrella, with the books and her speaker and money for lunch, while she went off with Nick and his group of surfer friends. I was always invited along, but I never went. They were only asking because they felt obligated, which made sense since they were all sixteen, seventeen, and eighteen, and I was only twelve.

At night Nina and I would lie in our beds in the room we were sharing, with the window opened and the warm salt air blowing in past the blue and white striped curtains. "Isn't it wonderful here?" she'd said one night. "Don't you just want to stay here forever?" But she was talking to herself then, not to me.

And that is how the summer passed.

The evening before we were set to go home, we packed our stuff and went to bed. In the middle of the night I awoke to the sound of Nina sneaking out. I still remember what she looked like climbing through the bedroom window in a white sundress, running across the lawn, her sun-bleached hair flying behind her as she went. I got up then, stood there at the window waving, but she never turned back to see.

She returned just before dawn, and cried quietly into her pillow. Somehow I knew I was supposed to pretend to be asleep.

# TWELVE

It's an hour later, and we're in the car, zooming west. I turn toward Sean, I still can't quite believe we're really doing this. "And you're *sure*?" I say. "I mean, you're *sure* you don't mind all this driving and everything?"

Sean shakes his head. "Ellie, I love driving. It's like playing the world's most realistic driving video game. And think of all the Frequent Driver miles I'm racking up for future trips."

"That's not a real thing," I say.

"Well okay, fine. But think," he turns toward me and grins, "after this you'll owe me." I blush and grin back.

I guess if there's one thing I have learned about the world, it's that things can always, always, always change. And those big changes often come a lot faster than you think. Less than three hours ago I was standing behind the counter at Mon Coeur feeling entirely alone. And now I'm in a car on my way to Nebraska with a cute guy I barely know.

Sean's phone buzzes. Sean reaches into his pocket, takes it out, and holds it to his ear. Through the back of the phone I hear a guy's voice calling out, "Hello? Hello? Hello?" Sean hangs up and tosses it onto the seat behind him. "Wrong number."

"How did you know it was a wrong number if you didn't even say hello?"

"I get them all the time. I'm pretty sure there's some girl out there who gives out my number to subpar dudes. Like ones with sores on their face or ones who don't even know the hide-and-seek rules."

But before I can respond, my phone starts buzzing.

"Maybe she gave out your number, too?" Sean says.

A picture of Amanda laughing flashes on my screen. "It's my friend. The one who thinks I should give up."

"So pick it up and tell her to piss off," Sean shrugs.

I laugh, even though I would never, ever do that to Amanda. I hit *Ignore*. Truth is, I'm worried that even hearing her voice will somehow break the spell that has made this all possible. Amanda has a way of bringing me back to earth, whether I want her to or not. But a second later, the phone buzzes again. And I realize she's going to keep calling over and over until I pick up. Amanda can be very persistent. And I guess can't avoid her forever.

I answer.

"Heeelleeeeeew," Amanda says. I can already tell she's drunk.

"Hey," I say. There's loud dance music pumping in the background.

"Ellieeeeeee? Sorry, honey, I can't hear you, hold on one second," and then she yells to someone in the background, "Can you turn it down please. Adam . . . can you? TURN IT DOWN A LITTLE PUH-LEASE!" and then into the phone, "Hey, babe! What are you doing?!!" And then, "I'M TALKING TO ELLIE, MY BESTEST BESTEST BESTEST!" And then, "Adam wants to know why you're not here."

"Who's Adam?" I hear a loud "woo-hoo" in the background.

"Adam is this total *jerk*." Amanda's laughing. "Eric never showed up but I DON'T EVEN CARE!"

And then there's a shuffling noise and a guy says into the phone "Hey, Ellie," and in the background Amanda yells, "GIVE THE PHONE BACK!!!" and then I hear her laughing.

"Hello," I say.

"What are you up to, how come you're not over here?" the guy asks.

And then more shuffling. "Sorry." Amanda's back. "He is *the worst*." More laughter. And then Amanda yells into the background, "YES! OF COURSE SHE'S HOT!" And then back to me, "How'd you get home from Mon Coeur?"

"Got a ride."

"From Brad? Brad's Thomas?"

"Sean drove me." She's waiting for me to explain. "No one you know," I say.

"Oh," she says. "Sorry, can you hold on a sec?" There's a shuffling sound and Amanda yells, "PUT ME DOWN, YOU BEHEEEEEEEEMOTH!!!" She's laughing still, and then she's back. "Well, where are you now?"

"In a car," I say.

"Where are you *going?*"

"To Nebraska." I glance at Sean. He waggles his eyebrows.

The music in the background gets louder. "WHAT DID YOU SAY?"

"I SAID I'M GOING TO NEBRASKA," I yell.

"GUYS, TURN IT DOWN I'M ON THE PHO-WOAH-N," Amanda yells. The noise in the background fades. "Hello? What did you say, Ellie?"

"I'm on my way to Nebraska," I say.

"*Ellie, what are you even talking about?*" Amanda sounds annoyed. "Nebraska isn't even a real place."

"I think it probably is, actually. I think I saw a picture online once."

"Well, not a real place anyone actually *goes* to."

"I'm going there," I say. "Right now."

"Okay, fine," Amanda says. "You're on your way to Nebraska, yeah, sure. Whatever, Ellie. I would have thought you'd stopped being weird by now, but I guess I was wrong."

"I'm not being weird," I say flatly. "I'm just telling you where I'm going."

"Wait, but . . . ," She sounds very serious, in a drunk sort of way. "*Why?*"

"Just because."

"*With who?*"

"Sean."

"Who is Sean?"

I turn toward Sean. "Sean, who are you?"

"A hide-and-seek champion slash coffee addict slash fantastic driver slash . . ."

"I mean *what's his last name?*"

"Sean, what's your last name?"

"You're going to *Nebraska* with a guy whose last name you don't even know?"

"Lerner," Sean says.

"Lerner," I say.

"Where does he go to school?"

"My friend Amanda wants to know where you go to school, Sean."

"Beacon Prep," Sean says. "Boarding school in Lake Forest for preppie rich kids."

I raise my eyebrows at him.

"Beacon Prep," I say into the phone. "Boarding school in Lake Forest for preppie rich kids."

"I know that place," Amanda says. "Mom's friend Helen's nephew goes there. Where do you know him from?"

"Sean, where do I know you from?" I hold up the phone.

"The future," Sean calls out.

"What?" says Amanda. "I couldn't hear you."

"I met him at the Mothership."

"You met a guy *there*? You didn't even tell me."

"I guess I forgot," I say. And then for a moment we are both silent.

"Alright," Amanda says. "Weeell . . . I guess I'll let you go then." She's pissed.

That makes two of us.

"Okay," I say.

"I hope you know what you're doing, Ellie," Amanda says. "Bye."

"Bye," I say. I lean back against my seat and watch the trees zip by.

"Well, that sounded fun," Sean says.

"She didn't seem to understand the concept of Nebraska."

The sun is going down now, and we are both quiet. I feel Sean looking at me, and when I turn he is all crazy grin and sparkling eyes. He rolls down his window and sticks his head out.

"HELL YEAH, NEBRASKA! Try it," he says.

I roll mine down, too. The wind rushes in, whipping my hair in my face.

"HOORAY, NEBRASKA!"

"GO, GO, NEBRASKA!"

"YAHOO, NEBRASKA!"

"WE KNOW YOU ARE REAL, NEBRASKA!"

The mood in the car has shifted, just like that.

# THIRTEEN

The rumble of the road beneath us becomes the soundtrack for a very long movie about cars on a long flat highway under a giant sky. I am lulled into a trance watching it.

Except for the road sounds, the car is silent, no music, no talking, but it's the kind of comfortable silence that only occurs between two people who are secure in the fact that they have plenty to say to each other. Which is funny because Sean and I have only spent a few hours in each other's presence.

Driving time always passes weird. The sky changes from clear blue to orange to pink to black. And then there is nothing but tiny car lights up ahead, and giant stretches of flat land on either side of us. Each time a car or a truck passes, I feel a little poke in my chest, like we are all part of some special club of people who are up late doing secret things, and I can't help but feel like somehow all of them must be looking for my sister, too.

Just after one in the morning, I spot a sign on the side of the highway showing a big slice of cherry pie with *Sweetie's Diner, All-American Roadside Favorite Open Round The Clock Since 1953.*

*World's Best Pancakes. Next Exit* written below. I cannot quite believe that we've really done this.

Sean gets off at the exit and circles around and then there, in the dark Nebraska night, is an enormous pink and silver diner with *sweetie's* written in orange neon lights at the top, the brightest thing for miles around. Sean pulls into the large parking lot. There are two other cars, three eighteen-wheelers with *Interstate Heavy Hauling* printed on the back, and one large bus with *MidAmerican Busline* written on the side and a big white 257 sign behind glass up above the windshield.

Sean parks. We get out.

The air feels cool and clear out here, and when I look up at the sky I remind myself that those tiny pinpoints of light up there are larger than I could ever even imagine, and that all that menacing blackness is actually nothing at all.

Sweetie's Diner feels instantly familiar the way all good diners do: It's all big giant booths and scratched chrome stools up at the counter, the scents of smoky bacon and burnt coffee. We blink under the bright lights like two people who have just been born.

My sister was in this very room, I think. I breathe in deep, as though some part of her is still here, and if I can catch it with my breath I'll get all the answers. But all I get is the smell of food. My stomach grumbles. Sean and I drove straight through dinner.

A woman with gray hair pulled back into a bun walks by with two plates balanced on each arm. "Sit wherever you like," she says.

Sean starts heading toward a booth in the back, looking around as he goes. Up at the wooden fans on the ceiling, down at the flecked linoleum tile floor. We pass a woman in her late twenties with a toddler asleep in her arms, an older couple sitting next to each other, sipping cups of tea, a man in his early thirties, slumped ever so slightly in his seat, his hand poised on his fork, his eyes closed, as though he's taking a nap but doesn't want anyone to know about it. Sean sits down in a booth and I slide in across from him. He opens his menu but stares out at nothing. "Sean?" I say.

Sean shakes his head. "Sorry." He smiles again. "We've been driving a long time, huh?"

A server approaches. She looks very awake considering how late it is, and she has a friendly face. Her name tag says *Rosie*.

"Hi there, what can I get for you, honeys?" Rosie says.

And I want to answer, "My missing sister, please!" but instead I just reach in my pocket for Nina's photograph. I am suddenly nervous. Sean is staring right at me with his beautiful slate-colored eyes, and when his eyes meet mine, I feel that same flash, now familiar, but still surprising in its intensity and the knot in my stomach loosens. Just a little.

I look up at Rosie. I hesitate for one more second, resting in this moment where anything is still possible, and then I open my mouth. "I was wondering if you or anyone who works here might have ever seen this girl." I put the photograph out on the table and slide it toward her. "She's my sister," I say. "She was here at least once . . ."

Before I even finish answering there's a squeezing in my chest.

And I suddenly realize what an idiot I've been. ". . . About two years ago."

I got caught up in the excitement of finding a piece of new information in the credit card statement, in finding someone willing to help me. Coming here, putting all that effort in, really made me feel like we were *doing* something and therefore were guaranteed to find the next clue. But just because you have sat in the car for hours and hours does not mean you're going to find anything if there isn't anything to find. We're at a diner in the middle of Nebraska where Nina once came two entire years ago. What did I *think* we'd find? Before Rosie even opens her mouth, I know what the answer is going to be.

She takes her glasses from a chain around her neck and puts them up on the tip of her nose. She stares down at Nina's picture, then back up at me. "I wish I could help you, doll, but . . ." I feel myself starting to sink. "But I can't say that I'd remember her unless she was a regular, and we don't get too many of those out here on the highway. Back when this place first opened, the head waitress was dating one of the bus drivers, so he'd stop in to see her whenever he was passing through, and then it became tradition for the bus company that does this route to use us as their rest stop. Really the only repeat customers we get are the bus drivers and the truckers." Rosie looks at Nina's picture one last time and hands it back to me, shaking her head. "It's a shame. Your sister's missing or something?" She asks this like someone who won't be surprised at the answer.

I nod. I can't speak or I'm afraid I'll cry.

"It's a real shame when that happens," Rosie nods. "You two really look alike, you know? If I didn't know you were looking for her and I saw this picture, I might think this was you. You know where she was headed or anything?"

I shake my head.

I look down at the beige tabletop, at the white and green Sweetie's place mat. The tears well up and I blink them back.

"Is there someone else we could talk to?" Sean asks. "Someone else who was working here back then who might have seen her?"

"Don't think so," Rosie says. "Of everyone, I've been here the longest. Most of the other girls started pretty recently. People don't usually last too long here."

I nod.

"Can I get you kids anything?"

"Three large iced coffees," Sean says. "And a grilled cheese."

"For you, hon?" I shake my head.

"You sure?" Sean says. "You must be hungry by now." His voice is soft and sweet. He reaches out and takes my hand.

"I'll have a grilled cheese, too, I guess," I say. Rosie nods and then walks away.

Sean leaves his hand on top of mine.

A minute later the three iced coffees arrive and a few minutes after that, our food.

Sean's phone starts vibrating on the table in front of us. "Pipe down!" he says to his phone. He holds one finger up to his lips as if to shush it, then smiles at me.

"Attention passengers on bus two fifty-seven." A short man in a navy blue uniform is standing up at the front of the diner. "We'll be leaving in five minutes," he calls out. "Five minutes! Anyone not on the bus will get left behind so I suggest if you haven't already settled up your checks that you do that right now." All around us people begin to gather up their belongings.

We continue eating in silence. Or rather, Sean eats and I sit there. It's late at night and we're so far from home. And now we are just two people sitting in a diner in the middle of Nebraska for, as it turns out, no reason at all. I look up at Sean. "Now what?" I ask him. Though I don't expect him to have the answer.

"Now we pay, and then we go find somewhere to crash for the night. And in the morning we figure out the next step." And Sean looks so determined and hopeful, so I nod even though I'm thinking that there *is* no next step. The next step is we go back home and I try and forget that I ever found Nina's drawing in the first place. "We're going to find her, Ellie," Sean says. "There's going to be another clue, okay? There will be. I know it. But if you give up now, you might not be able to see it even if it's right in front of you."

I stare down at my plate. I am suddenly so very, very tired. Sean takes the last sip of his second iced coffee and puts the cup back down. He points to the third. "There are ideas in there. Brilliant ideas that are going to blow your mind. All I have to do is drink it and then I will tell you what they are."

I try and smile. This trip was a failure and we both know it. It's sweet that he's still trying but that doesn't change the facts. I am pretty much definitely about to cry.

85

"I'll be right back," I say. I get up. "I'm going to the bathroom."

I feel Sean watching me as I walk toward the back. I push through the door. Every surface in the bathroom is covered in graffiti — the walls, the sinks, the floor, the ceiling, the toilets, the paper towel dispenser, the trash can, the windows. *Jack loves Sarah* is written on the outside of one of the stalls in thick black marker. And there's *AJ and CJ forever* in pink right near my foot. There's *Lindsay and Jeanine* next to a picture of two sets of lips, kissing on one side of the garbage can. And on the other side of the garbage can there's *SP would never toss TM in the trash!*

A woman comes out of one of the stalls, sniffling, eyes red and puffy. "Don't believe any of it," she says. I turn around.

"Sorry?"

She blows her nose loudly on a piece of toilet paper.

"All that stuff people on those buses say about that first bus driver and the first diner waitress when this place first opened and their special love and blah-blah-blah and how because of them this bathroom is all magical and whatever, and how people love each other forever after they write their names together on the wall? Don't believe any of it." She bends down and points to a spot on the floor, which reads *Driggs loves Annie*. "It's all crap." She reaches into her back pocket and produces a dark-purple Sharpie. She crosses out the *loves Annie* and replaces it with *has a skinny penis.* She looks up at me. "It's true, you know. Like a Twizzler." Then she puts the cap back on and walks out.

I am alone again, staring at the wall. I pee. I look at the mirror over the sink while I'm washing my hands. It's so covered in scribbles it's almost impossible to see myself.

And right there in the center of the mirror above one of the sinks is a simple line drawing of a guy's face — strong jaw, wide mouth, big eyes — and right there in that familiar graceful curved script, *Cakey ❤'s J.*

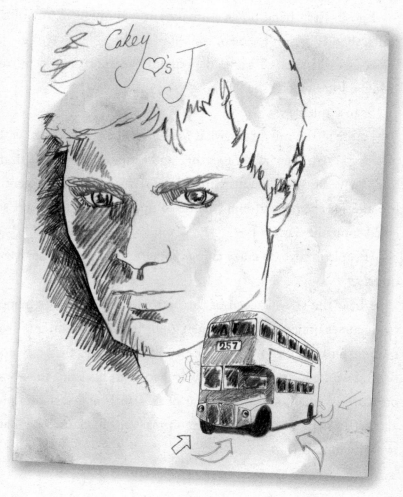

I reach out and touch the mirror. The glass is cool, but the letters feel hot under my skin, like they're alive. I can barely breathe.

*Nina.*

I race back to our table where Sean is draining the last sip of coffee number three.

"I found something."

And I grab Sean's hand and drag him toward the bathroom.

I go in first, bend down to make sure no one is in any of the stalls, then I motion for Sean to follow me.

"Nina did this," I say and point to the spot on the mirror. "Maybe I know why she left now."

Sean is silent.

I stare at the mirror for what feels like a very long time as the pieces connect themselves together and a story forms itself in my brain. My sister had an entire life I knew nothing about. An entire life and an entirely different name to go along with it. And she loved someone named J.

"People in love do crazy things sometimes, I guess," Sean says quietly.

I hear the slow screech of the bathroom door creaking open. Sean curses under his breath, then grabs my arm and in one swift motion pulls me into one of the stalls and shuts the stall door behind us. I can smell him, the warm scent of his skin, the grease on his lips. His body is radiating heat. I feel his heart pumping against mine. I start to laugh for no reason. He clamps his hand over my mouth.

We hear the *click-click-click* of a woman's shoes tapping against the tile floor, the rush of the faucet and then the creak of the door opening back up. "You don't have to hide, you know," a woman calls on the way out. "You think you're the first two people to come in here together?" And then the door creaks shut.

Sean looks down at me, and I feel myself blushing. We leave the stall, go back to the sink. My mouth is still warm where his hand was. I look at Nina's drawing on the mirror one last time, trace the lines she drew with the tip of my finger, following the path she must have followed with her pen. And I notice something that I hadn't noticed before, there next to the mirror, drawn on as though it is driving up the side, is a little bus, drawn by Nina, with a tiny picture of herself in the window, and three little numbers written on the front: *257.*

I hold on to Sean's arm. I point, suddenly breathless with my own realization. Our eyes meet. And then I am grabbing Sean's hand, or maybe he is grabbing mine, and we are running back through the dining room, which is almost completely empty now. Through the front window we can see bus 257 pulling away. Sean takes out his wallet, tosses a couple twenties onto our table, and together we tumble out into the night.

# FOURTEEN

We run, our feet slapping against the pavement, and fling ourselves into the car. Sean peels out of the parking lot, and we catch up to the bus right before it pulls out onto the highway. It is only once we are safely situated behind its giant chrome bumper that Sean turns to me and shakes his finger, saying, "Well, see? I told you so! There'd be a clue! A clue for which I have now decided to give myself full credit."

"Thank you," I say. I lean back against the seat. I'm not tired anymore. It's not an I've-gone-to-sleep-and-woken-up kind of awake, it's an all-this-adrenaline-has-shifted-me-over-to-a-different-reality kind of awake. I sit back up. "Seriously, thank you for everything, for all of this."

"Eh, don't mention it. I have ulterior motives."

I feel my face getting hot. "Oh?"

"Yeah," he says. "Because there's nothing I can do to find my brother. So going with you on this trip makes me feel like, I don't know, like I'm *doing* something."

My stomach tightens.

"For siblings everywhere!" He punches the air, like he's trying to make things light, but his smile doesn't reach his eyes.

"I'm so sorry," I say. "I wasn't thinking about how this must . . ."

"Don't." Sean turns toward me and puts his hand on my arm. "It's nice that you want to, but you don't need to." My skin feels hot where he's touching it. "We're the same, you and me." Something is happening in the car, the energy is changing in here. I hold my breath. We sit there like that, his hand still on my arm, his fingers moving ever so slightly. And then suddenly he takes his hand away.

He clears his throat. "So she was full of surprises, huh?"

I miss his hand. I want him to put his hand back. I shift in my seat.

"Your sister I mean. She was *surprising*." For a second I feel protective of Nina, which doesn't make any sense of course. Sean only knows what I've told him. And what I've told him certainly doesn't make her sound like a rock of reliability.

Sean is looking straight ahead. His face glows red from the taillights in front of us. I lean back and close my eyes. The images flash through my brain — the ink on the mirror, the guy's face, the heart, at once comforting and terrible. Comforting because she was okay, she was happy. She was in love. Terrible because she left us all for a guy and she never looked back. "Yeah," I say. "I guess she was."

*     *     *

Maybe there was a sign and I missed it.

A month or so before Nina disappeared, I had gone into her room to find a pencil, or that is what I told myself I was doing to have an excuse to snoop without feeling bad about it. The few months prior, Nina hadn't been around much. The house felt different when she wasn't there, like no matter how many lights I'd turn on, it was always too dark.

I remember pushing her door open and how the room smelled like her, like the ginger and orange perfume she always wore. There were jeans and tank tops tossed on the floor and the bed, a few bottles of hair dye on the desk, and just like always, drawings everywhere: on the walls, on the desk, on the floor, on the dresser, on her bed, torn up, crumpled, folded, some perfectly finished, some she'd only just begun. I remember examining a row of detailed little portraits and wondering if they were all faces she'd made up in her head, or if her life was populated by a whole world of people who I'd never even seen before.

There were the pencils in a can on the desk. I grabbed one and let myself glance around her room one more time. There on the floor was a half crumpled piece of paper covered in tiny handwriting. I poked it with my toe, hoping to "accidentally" get it to uncurl so I could read it. I dropped my pencil and bent down to pick it up. I looked at the paper again, *I love you* was written on it over and over and over in blue ballpoint pen. The marks were extra dark, whoever had written the letter had pushed so hard with their pen that it had torn the paper in a few places, because that's how much they meant it. I stared at that paper, and tried to imagine what it would feel like to be Nina, to be so loved by everyone, that one individual person's love could mean so little to you. That you could toss it on the floor. I felt a stab of something then, similar to jealousy, but not jealousy exactly, mixed with a little twinge of pity for whoever had written the letter. I remember having an urge to pick that letter up, to smooth it out and take it to my room, to pretend it had been written just for me.

For the next six hours, the view out the front window doesn't change — six red circles, four enormous wheels, a big chrome bumper. I might think we hadn't moved at all, except for the fact that when we started driving, it was dark, and now the sun has risen, turning the sky the cool light blue of morning. And the bus has finally stopped, on a side-street bus depot. And now here we are in Denver, Colorado.

The buildings are far apart and the streets are wide. There's a giant dome of open sky over us, reminding us that the city is not all there is.

The bus door opens and a line of dazed and sleepy-looking passengers emerge. A girl a couple years older than I am comes off the bus and claims her sagging red duffel bag from the pile of luggage on the sidewalk. Two years ago, this could have been Nina. The girl turns around; she seems like she's looking for someone, like she's worried they might not be here. I feel like I'm watching a movie about the past and the part of Nina is being played by this girl. I catch her eye and she smiles and I'm weirdly relieved, as though if this girl is okay, it means Nina was, too. This makes no sense.

I think *I am very, very tired*. I think *maybe it is time to lie down now*. I turn toward Sean who is leaning back against the seat, eyes half-closed. Suddenly I'm picturing the two of us together in a bed, my cheek resting against his chest.

I force myself to look away and concentrate on what's in front of me. What I see now is what my sister saw two years ago — this wide street, tall gray stone buildings, lush green trees. I step out of the car. What was in her head when she walked down the stairs of the bus onto this sidewalk? Joy? Relief? Excitement? Sadness? I breathe in the clear morning air and try to imagine what it would feel like to be Nina arriving in this very spot. I reach up and touch my hair, imagine it ocean blue. I stand up straight and tip my head slightly back the way Nina always did. I close my eyes. When I open them, I notice there's a slightly crumbling community bulletin board in a grassy clearing about fifteen feet away, placed as to be directly in the line of vision of anyone getting off the bus. I head toward it. It's covered in colored flyers: ads for a cheap motel, for restaurants and coffee houses, for rooms for rent. And up at the very top of the bulletin board are a few permanent ads behind glass. *Rocky Mountain Tours — See Denver With the People Who Know It Best* and *Keep Denver Beautiful — Get a Tattoo at Bijoux Ink. 2740 Colfax Avenue.*

I touch the thick glass.

Bijoux. As in "Bijoux, wheere aaaaare yooou?" And I know it seems crazy, but I suddenly feel like I can imagine exactly how it must have gone: Nina was standing here, new to this city, fresh off a fifteen-hour bus ride, and she reached out and she touched this sign, just like I'm doing now. In a city of unfamiliar people and unfamiliar things, this sign comforted her, she saw this and she thought *yes*. I feel this yes coursing through my body as if it were coming from inside me. Maybe I think this because of some special connection I still have to my sister. Maybe after all this time the strength of our bond can cross space and time and I can understand one thought she might have had, even though I cannot understand them all.

Or maybe I just think this because of how tired I am, and because of how very badly I want this to be true.

I guess there's only one way to find out.

# FIFTEEN

But first, we need sleep.

Sean and I drive to the closest motel, a run-down place that rents rooms by the hour. And now the woman behind the counter stands in front of us, the room key dangling from her skinny index finger. "And you're sure you kids are over eighteen, right?" She raises one heavily penciled eyebrow and nods slowly.

"Of course," Sean says, nodding back.

"Okay, good." She hands him a key on a white plastic Travel Route Inn key chain. "Checkout is at eleven. Continental breakfast is served until nine . . . if you're up by then." And then she smirks like she knows something about why we're here and what we're up to. And even though what she thinks she knows is wrong, I blush.

We walk back outside, up a small set of concrete stairs and into the room. It smells like mold in here, and someone's bad breath. There are two twin beds covered in sad floral comforters and in between them there's a small chipped nightstand and above the small nightstand is a framed picture of what I think is supposed to be a pineapple made by someone who has obviously never seen one.

"Honey, we're home," Sean says. He pulls back the covers on one of the beds and crawls in, still wearing all his clothes. Before I've even taken off my shoes, I can tell from his breathing, slow and rhythmic, that he's asleep. I look over at him. His lips are parted and his face is relaxed. His eyelashes brush against his cheeks. My heart squeezes. He looks different to me now, just ever so slightly different than he did yesterday. I cannot explain this and I don't understand it. All I know is in this moment, I feel like I could sit here and watch him all day. But instead I change into some of the clothes I tossed into the bag with me last night and force myself to get in bed. Within minutes, I am sleeping, too.

# SIXTEEN

I have a version of that dream again, the one I used to have all the time after Nina first disappeared. In the dream I go into the third bedroom in our apartment and there's a girl in there, sitting at a desk. I ask her who she is. How did she get in here? What does she want? But the girl doesn't answer, she just laughs like I'm making a joke. And she thinks this joke is very funny. And I am so weirdly proud at making this strange girl laugh that I don't tell her that my questions were serious.

And then the girl says, "Oh, Belly," and I realize the girl is Nina. She has a different haircut than when she vanished; her hair is made of thin strands of real gold and I decide that's probably why I didn't recognize her at first. But where has she been the last two years? I ask. She shakes her head like I am crazy. Why, she's been here, of course! And I am confused, so confused, but Nina shrugs and smiles. She asks me if I want to go through her clothes and help her pick out what would work best with her new haircut, and I say okay and she opens this door in her bedroom that I hadn't noticed before, which opens into a giant warehouse, filled up to the ceiling with beautiful things. Right near the door there's a giant bunch of gold Mylar balloons on extra long strings. She tells me she's been selling them to make extra money, which is how she could afford all the new clothes. Normally she charges two hundred and fifty-seven dollars for each balloon. But I can have as many as I want, all for free, because I'm her sister. She begins walking around the enormous closet, gathering up the balloons for me. But then the balloons start to lift her up off the floor and each time she adds to her collection she rises a little higher. She doesn't seem to notice, or if she does, she doesn't care. I look up at the ceiling and now it's nothing but sky. And she is still gathering those balloons, going up and up and up. And I am yelling, "Nina, stop!" and "Nina, let go!" but she isn't listening. "Nina, stop! Nina, stop!" I yell louder and louder. And this is usually how the dream ends, with me screaming and her rising higher and higher and higher until I can't see her anymore. Only this time, it's different. This time, right when she is about to pass between where the room ends and where the sky begins, she does let go and starts to fall. Faster and faster, she hurtles toward the ground. And I am terrified, because I do not know if I will be able to catch her.

I wake up just after one-thirty in the afternoon, staring at Sean's dimly lit naked back. He's by the sink in the corner, wet from a shower, a thin motel towel wrapped around his waist. I can see his reflection in the mirror — his smooth chest, the faint line of hair leading down his stomach. He raises a smaller towel up to his head and starts rubbing his hair, in the mirror his biceps are flexing and releasing, flexing and releasing. There's something on the inside of his upper arm, a smattering of white jagged lines. Scars. From an accident maybe? I wonder. I want to reach out and touch them.

When he begins to take his towel off, I force myself to squeeze my eyes shut, and behind my eyelids I picture what I'm not seeing. I breathe, in and out, trying to lie perfectly still.

"Ellie, wake uuuuuuupp."

"Mmmpph?" I open my eyes again. This time Sean is standing right in front of me, barefoot but fully clothed, his cheeks flushed from the steam of the shower.

"You sleep cute." Sean says. And then he flips on the light. I sit up in bed, swing my feet over the edge. The moment they hit the floor, my phone starts vibrating on the nightstand.

Without even thinking, I pick it up.

"Oh my God, what is going *on*? I've called you like a hundred times in a row!" It's Amanda.

"Huh?" I'm too groggy from sleep to deal with this right now.

"That guy? Sean? Are you still with him?"

"Hi, Amanda," I say.

"I've been calling you," she says. "Why didn't you call me back?"

Sean sits down at the end of the bed.

"I was busy," I say. And I glance at Sean, who is leaning over putting on his socks.

"Ellie. Helen was over here this morning picking my mom up for Pilates and she called her nephew Bryce from our house, you

100

know, the one who goes to Beacon, and Bryce said one of his friends used to room with Sean and that Sean's a total freak."

I glance at Sean. He is tying his shoes now.

"I'm not sure anyone in Helen's family is really in a place to make that kind of judgment," I say. Helen is Amanda's mom's friend, a woman who I'm pretty sure gets a new nose put on her face every other year at Christmastime. An actual new nose. Like from surgery.

"I'm serious. Bryce says he doesn't have any friends at school and sits around by himself all the time, like staring at things. And also I think he has a girlfriend."

"What?!" The word pops out. My insides twist.

"Yeah, Bryce said Sean keeps a picture of some girl in a frame next to his bed and he basically makes out with it every night before he goes to sleep. And he's always writing letters late at night, like love letters to her or something."

"I don't know what you expect me to say to that. I mean, I doubt that's even true, and . . ." I pause. "What do you expect me to say to that?"

"That you're ditching the weirdo with the girlfriend and coming back home immediately."

"But I'm not going to do that."

"I don't get it, what are you even *doing* in Nebraska?"

"We're not there anymore."

"Then where are you?"

"Denver."

"Why would you be in Denver?"

"Why wouldn't I be?"

"Ellie, have you been kidnapped or something? If you've been kidnapped, cough twice."

"I'm not even going to humor that with a response," I say. If she were genuinely worried, I might feel bad, but she doesn't sound worried at all. Actually, she sounds kind of jealous. "And I'm not really even sure why you called, actually."

"You're not *sure* why I called? Um, hi, I'm your friend and everything you're doing right now is pretty insane. Why don't you come home now, Ellie? I'm seeing this new guy, Adam, and he has a friend, Cody, and I think he'd be perfect for you, Ellie. *Come home.*"

She says this like it's a command. Like she has the right to make such commands. I shake my head.

Sean has both shoes on now, and he stands up and walks back to the bathroom.

"I have to go now," I say.

"No wait, listen . . ." Amanda says. But before she finishes her sentence, I've already hung up.

# SEVENTEEN

It's hot out now and there's this manic energy in the air, like we're bubbles in a liquid that's about to boil. Sean is walking fast and I'm right behind him, heading down Colfax Avenue.

The street is full and we're dodging people as we go. Two girls are walking toward us. They're wearing these flimsy little sundresses and the sun is behind them, so you can see basically everything. They're staring at Sean. One whispers something to the other and waggles her eyebrows. The blush rushes to my face. I stare at the back of Sean's head to see if he's noticed them but I can't tell.

"Hey, Sean?" He doesn't turn around. My phone starts buzzing in my pocket and I glance at it — Amanda. I hit *Ignore*. Sean has stopped walking now. A couple feet away a guy with a million tattoos is leaning against a storefront talking on the phone.

"I think this is it," Sean says, pausing now, looking back.

We push through the door. No one looks up. It's loud inside, with punk music blasting over the whirring of an air conditioner. There's a giant gold-and-crystal chandelier hanging from the ceiling, the kind of thing you'd see in a fancy hotel lobby or at the opera. To the right, two black leather couches are packed with people flipping through black binders. To the left is a huge glass case filled with jewelry — thick steel barbells, swirling ebony ear spacers, delicate gold hoops with captured rubies. There's a dark gray curtain against the back wall, and a woman walks through it. She has choppy black hair and a fierce shark underbite. There's a thick green snake inked all the way around her neck, its head resting on her collarbone, a bright red apple in its mouth.

Shark taps the big black tablet in front of her.

"Sandrine Miller," she calls out. Her voice is slightly hoarse like she probably spends a lot of time yelling.

A tiny purple-haired girl rises from one of the couches, makes an exaggerated "I'm-so-nervous" face to her purple-haired friend, and then heads into the back room. Sean and I make our way up to the front.

"Hi," I say. Over Shark's shoulder I can see into the other room. Sandrine Miller is leaning back on what looks like a big leather dentist's chair and pulling up her shirt. A guy with a pink crew cut is getting ready to pierce her nipple. A few feet away, a girl with a pile of black curls tied in a knot on top of her head is applying a tattoo transfer onto the giant arm of a biker dude. Shark catches me watching and shoots me a nasty glare.

A dark-haired guy pops his head out from behind the curtain. "Eden?" He sounds scared. "Um, did the fourteen-gauge needles come in with the last shipment?"

"Should be in the back if Cedar put the order in."

"I'll keep looking."

"If she forgot to order them . . ." Shark/Eden, shakes her head. "That girl's time has about run out."

"We were really busy all week while you were away," the guy says. Shark/Eden raises one eyebrow and the guy shrinks. "I should have reminded her."

"Ron, just because she screwed you once doesn't mean you have to take the blame for her. Stop being such a sucker. When you're done with that client, you're going to watch the front. I'm going to have to head out to find us some."

He winces slightly, then pulls his head back through the curtain.

Shark/Eden turns back toward us. "You don't look eighteen," she says.

"I'm not here for a tattoo," I say.

"Oh?" She crosses her arms.

"I'm looking for my sister," I say. "Her name is Nina Wrigley and I was wondering if she had ever come in here. It would have been a while ago, two years maybe, but maybe if I showed you a picture of her, you'd recognize her?"

Shark/Eden's expression is completely unchanged, almost like she hasn't heard me. She glances at Sean, then back at me.

"So," I say. "Can I show you her picture? Maybe see if you remember her? She might have been here with a guy or something . . ."

A muscle twitches in her jaw, but she still doesn't say anything. I take Nina's photo from my pocket, hold it out. "This is her."

I watch Shark/Eden's face. There are deep lines around her mouth and creases between her eyebrows, like she's so sure that something is about to make her mad that she's making a mad face in advance. But when her eyes focus on Nina's picture, her expression softens. Just for a second, she looks like someone else. And then she shakes her head. "Don't know her," Eden says. "Sorry." She shrugs, she turns around and starts walking away, then she stops, turns back. "Please don't stand here at the counter, this space is for customers." And then she disappears into the back.

"Dammit," Sean whispers under his breath.

He's making his way toward the door, shaking his head. I am frozen.

I look back at Shark/Eden and she's watching us. Sean comes back, grabs my arm. "Let's go," he whispers. This doesn't seem right. Something just isn't right here.

Back out in the bright sunlight, I turn toward Sean.

"I think she's lying," I say.

Sean stops, his lips part slightly. He cocks his head.

"About her not knowing Nina, I mean." As I hear myself say it, I become more sure.

"Reeeeeally." The word oozes slowly from Sean's mouth, and by the time he's done, he's grinning. "What makes you say that?"

"This is going to sound crazy," I say.

"All the best ideas do."

"It was the expression that was on her face when she looked at Nina's picture. It was . . . sort of soft and sweet I guess? Like she was a little bit amused and also she wanted to take care of Nina, like she was looking at the picture of Nina the way people sometimes looked at Nina, the person. Which makes me think she not only met her, she actually *knew* her." I bite my bottom lip. "But, then, why would she lie about that? Was she trying to pro — "

"So where do you want to get lunch then?" Sean says loudly. He puts his arm around my waist and pulls me close. Eden is passing right by us going fast up the hill. Sean keeps his arm around me until she's gone.

"Maybe she's just one of those people who likes to be in control," Sean says softly. "Wants to be the one with all the power."

"Screw that," I say. "I'm going back in there." I turn around and start walking.

"To do what?" Sean calls out behind me.

"I don't know. Look around I guess. I'll figure it out when I get there."

I push back through the door. Sandrine Miller is now standing in front of the couch talking to her friend. "No, seriously," she's saying. She has her pointer finger looped inside the neckline of her clingy tank top and is holding it out away from her body. "It was like two little pinches. I'm sure Kate's bitten them harder a billion times! You should do it. We'll be nipple-twins!" She leans forward so her friend can see down her shirt. "Look how cute!"

I walk up to the register. The dark-haired guy, Ron, is at the front counter. He's leaning against it, reading a magazine called *Terminal Ink*. On the front cover is a picture of a girl covered in tattoos and wearing a black forties-style bathing suit.

He is nodding at the magazine, like it's suggesting something to him that he agrees with.

Behind him the curtain is opened ever so slightly. I need to get back there.

"I'm interested in a tattoo," I blurt out.

He looks up. "Weren't you in here like a second ago? Talking to Eden?"

"I was," I say. "I was going to get one but I got scared." I bite my bottom lip, an exaggerated expression of coy embarrassment. "Y'know, needles, yikes!" I hold up my hands. "I *really* want one though." I'm making this up as I go along, but it seems right somehow.

"First one?" he asks. I nod. "You have a design in mind?"

"Um . . . nope." I shrug. "I'll figure it out when I'm back there."

Ron eyes me suspiciously.

"I'm crazy like that!" I say.

"We like crazy here," he says and he starts to smile. "But, Crazy, here's a question, are you eighteen? Do you have ID?"

I reach into my back pocket and take out Nina's passport. Before I even have time to think about it, I've opened it up and slapped it onto the counter. Ron picks it up, looks at it, then back at me, then at the picture again. I hold my breath and try to make my most Nina-esque face, flirty and warm, and at the same time totally unconcerned. I think I end up looking deranged, but it doesn't even matter apparently, because Ron is nodding.

"Okay. Nina." Ron nods. He hands me back her passport. "I

liked your hair better the other way," he says. "Pink like in the picture."

"Me, too," I say. A weird part of me is kind of enjoying this. "I had to dye it back to normal when I got my job."

"Oh?" Ron asks. "What's that?"

"I'm a bartender," I say.

"Where?"

"Um . . . New York!" I'm digging myself deeper. I don't even know why. Do bartenders in New York *need* regular-colored hair? That seems unlikely. "The place I work is very fancy!" I blurt out.

"Cool cool," Ron says. "My buddy owns a rock-and-roll bar there, in Bushwick. Lipsink, but spelled with two *i*'s like *sink*."

"Oh of cooourse," I say, nodding. "Lipsink."

I turn back and look at Sean who's standing a few feet behind me. He winks, and the Nina in me winks right back.

Ron leads me behind the curtain. "Nina, meet Petra." He motions to a girl with long black hair held off her face by a thick red headband. She's big and curvy and gorgeous. She's wearing a paper-thin white tank top and a bunch of heavy bracelets on each wrist. Both arms are covered in tattoos. "Petra, Nina. Petra's the best," Ron says. "We stole her a month ago from the biggest tattoo shop in Nashville. She'll help you pick something out." He looks up at Petra. "Nina here is a virgin," he says. And then he walks back out into the front.

"So." Petra's grinning. "First one, huh?"

"Yup." I nod. "I decided what the hell, y'know?"

"Oh, do I!" Her grin widens. "Five years ago I was fresh as a brand-new baby. Then one day I was bored and had just ended a relationship and was thinking about how I'm always either in love with someone or missing someone so I got this." She taps the outline of a red heart on her bicep. There's a dashed red line in the middle and underneath in tiny script letters is written *your name goes here.* "But be careful, they're addictive!"

I nod and she winks.

"I'll go get the books," Petra says. "And maybe you'll get inspired." Petra walks away and I'm left sitting in the leather tattoo chair. Off to the side the girl with the black curls is tattooing the biker who has his eyes squeezed shut. I gaze around the room: There are shelves full of latex gloves, disposable needles, antibiotic cream. There's a cart full of cotton swabs and alcohol wipes, and hung all over the brick walls are dozens of framed photos. I stand up to get a closer look at a huge one right across from the chair. It's of three women and two men, all wearing cowboy hats. Petra is standing in the middle, beaming. Suddenly the real Petra's standing behind me. "They're Saddle Up Susie, big in Nashville," she says. "I know, no one up here's ever heard of them . . . but they were passing through town two weeks ago. I absolutely love them. My first pic on the wall of fame."

"Cool," I say.

Petra hands me a thick black binder. "Take a look at this one, I'll go get the others." She disappears down a small staircase. I keep looking at the photos and realize I recognize a bunch of the people in the pictures: a giant-eyed fashion model that Amanda says looks like a lizard, an artist famous for their political graffiti, an action star from the 90s, all standing with their tattoo artists, showing off their new tattoos.

I stop in front of one photo in the corner and freeze, my heart thumping in my chest.

There, in the photo, is my sister. She's with three guys in their early twenties. Two of the guys have red hair and red goatees and they're pointing at a third dark-haired guy whose pants are pulled partway down to reveal a giant tattoo on his lower stomach right below his belly button. The tattoo is a stylized picture of the faces of the other two, surrounded by musical notes. *Nina did this.* The tattooed guy has one arm around her shoulders. Her mouth is curved into a smile but she's looking far off into the distance. At the bottom of the photo is a scrawly signature, but it's impossible to make out what it says.

I turn around. The curly-haired girl is hunched over the biker's arm, whose eyes are still clamped closed. I grab the framed photo off the wall and flip it over. I use my fingernail to pry up the three metal pieces holding the photo in place. I shake the cardboard out and grab the photograph. I lift the front of my T-shirt, push the edge of the photograph down my cutoffs, and pull my T-shirt down over it. I drop the now empty frame behind a black metal cart just as Petra comes back into the room, holding a big stack of black photo albums. She holds them out toward me expectantly.

"See anything you like?" she says.

"I think I changed my mind again," I say. "I don't think I want a tattoo after all."

"Really?"

111

I shake my head. "Sorry," I say. And then I remind myself that I'm Nina. "I can be a little impulsive sometimes, I guess." I shrug and give her this big radiant smile, just like Nina would have. Petra smiles back, and then I turn and head back into the main room.

Sean is standing by the door. I grab his arm and drag him outside.

"What happened?"

"Keep walking." I lead us outside and up the hill, and only when we're five full blocks away do I stop and take the photo out from under my shirt.

"She actually *worked* there." I hand the photo to Sean. "Look."

"Whoa! This is amazing." He looks up at me. "Who are the dudes?"

"I don't know, but that's what we need to find out. Petra called the photo wall 'the wall of fame,' and I recognized a lot of the other people up on it, so I guess they must be at least kind of famous. I'm thinking maybe they're in a band because of the music notes?"

Sean is nodding. "You know who knows an awful lot of stuff about guys in bands?"

"People who want to do it with guys in bands?"

Sean takes his phone out of his pocket and starts typing. "Well, yeah," he says, without looking up. "But also, people who work in hip'n'trendy music stores who think they're going to get to do it with the people who want to do it with the guys in the bands by knowing about them . . ." Sean holds his phone out and points to a spot on the map three blocks away. Then looks up at me and grins. "Let's go."

Bottom Forty is a little pocket of anytime in the middle of this sunny summer day.

It could be any time of day in here, any time of year, any decade really. Music posters cover the windows, blocking out most of the outside light, and the air smells sweet, like incense mixed with something else. A woman rapping in French plays loudly over the sound system.

The guy behind the counter is about our age, wearing a white T-shirt with *ASK ME ABOUT MY DUCK* written on it in black Sharpie.

Sean takes the photo up to the front. The guy nods at Sean the way people do when they think they've spotted one of their own.

"Hey, man," Sean says. "Can you help me out here? I'm trying to figure out who the band in this picture is." He slides the photo across the counter.

"That's Monster Hands, of course." He looks up at Sean. "You seriously didn't know?"

"I'm not from around here," Sean says.

The guy shrugs, then hands the picture back to Sean. "Well, they're really disturbingly good. The guys are from Ireland but they got their start here in Denver, then got signed a couple years ago by this tiny indie label and have been touring pretty much solid for the last two years or so. Really dedicated cult following. You should check them out. Their last release is over there in the *M*s." The guy points. "Their new one's out in a few months."

The guy glances at me, as if to see if I'm impressed by how much he knows.

Sean and I walk toward the back. There's a guy and a girl standing in front of the *M*s, both about the same height, with straight, shiny, copper-colored hair. They both have pale clear skin, piggy looking upturned noses, and giant eyes, like they're from another planet where this is just how people look. The girl has her hand in the guy's back pocket. Sean reaches for the *M*s.

"Looking for Monster Hands?" The guy is watching me. "I heard you up at the front."

"Yeah," I say.

"Sorry, honeys," the girl says. She's holding up an album with a photo on the front of a giant monster hand holding a coffee cup. "Last one's ours."

"Can we see it for a second?" I ask.

"I know that trick!" The girl shakes her head. "We let you see it for a second and then you hightail it out of here. Nice try, though. People get very snatchy-snatchy when it comes to Monster Hands records. That's why we have to get this replacement. Because a friend, well, an *ex*-friend of ours stole our last one." The girl frowns. "Awww, you are so disappointed. Awww. Seriously. I can relate. Me and boyfi *looove* Monster Hands, don't we, babes?"

Her boyfriend nods at my boobs. "We love them."

"We cannot *wait* until their new album comes out. We're going to camp out in line like a week before. We already bought the tent and . . ." the girl stops and lets out a high-pitched squeal. "NO WAY!" She drops the album and snatches the photo of Nina and Monster Hands from Sean. "Oh my God. I'm pooing in my pants. I'm pooing in my pants right now! They got the Bijoux picture of Ian's tattoo! Can you believe it?!?" She waves the picture in her boyfriend's face.

"How the hell did you get this?" he says. "That lady who works in there is a *beast*! She could snap your leg in half with that jaw of hers."

I shrug.

"*Bad ass*," the guy says. He makes devil horns with his pinky and pointer fingers. The girl glares at me, then links her arm through his and pulls him close.

"But seriously though, the people in the Monster Hands group will pee their pants over this. Every single one of them in unison the second they see this." She shakes the photo around a little. She has green ink caked around each fingernail. "Okay. How much do you want for it?" She brushes her bangs to the side with her hand. She's wearing so much eyeliner.

"I'm not selling it," I say.

"Okay. I see what you're getting at. I can respect that." The girl nods. She takes a deep breath and then forces her mouth into a fake-looking smile. "I'm Jamie," she says. "And this is my boyfriend, Jamie. I know, Jamie and Jamie, so adorable, right? And what are your names?"

"I'm Ellie," I say.

"I'm Sean," he says.

"Well, Ellie and Sean, I understand why something like that might not be for sale, however, you must be open to a trade, right? Any reasonable person would be." Jamie-girl reaches into Jamie-boy's back pocket and takes out a duct tape wallet. She opens his wallet and removes a folded piece of paper. She leans in toward me. "Okay, like the fact that I am even showing you this is a big deal and seriously there are people who would pay serious cash for a tiny peek at this but . . ." She unfolds the paper, glances to her left and her right. "There. There it is. This is the drawing

that's going to be on the cover of their new album." She holds it out in front of her with a proud smirk on her face.

I raise my hand up to my mouth, inhale sharply. My heartbeat starts playing in fast-forward.

There in the center of the paper is a photocopy of a drawing — a girl with her hands on her head, her feet spread apart, her head tipped back, screaming.

"Oh my God," I whisper. "Where'd you get this?"

"We're really well-connected," Jamie-girl says. And then she shrugs to show how chill she's being about all of this.

"Do you know the person who drew this?" Sean is pressed against my arm. His heart is pounding, too.

"Nah. No idea," Jamie-girl shrugs again. "This is a copy of course, we keep the real one locked up. But if you'll give me that photo, I'll let you have this."

I stare at the drawing, I can barely even process what she's saying as my mind opens up to hold all this new information. Nina wasn't just some girl who tattooed them. She was probably someone they knew. Might still know. They might even know where she is.

"I need to meet them," I say. I look up. Jamie-guy is still watching me, his tongue protruding ever so slightly from between his chapped lips.

Jamie-girl lets out a snorty little laugh. "Well, unless you have a way to get to Phoenix by tomorrow night, that's not gonna happen anytime soon. That's the last show of their American tour before they go to Europe for two months." She takes the drawing and folds it back up and puts it back in Jamie-boy's wallet, which she then puts back into his pocket. "If you're such big Monsties, how come you don't already know all this?" I'm about to explain that really we're just looking for my sister, but before I can say anything, Sean starts talking.

"We heard them for the first time the other day," he says. "But right away it was like one of those things where you just really

118

connect to the music. You know how it is." Sean turns toward me and winks. "So, what about this Phoenix show tomorrow night? Where exactly is it?"

"This very hip and cool underground place that doesn't technically have a name," Jamie-boy says. "But everyone calls it Spit Pavilion, because it's really dusty out there in the desert and the dust makes everyone have to spit all the time. It's intense."

"You've been there?" Sean asks.

"Well . . . no, but we read all about it on our online group," Jamie-girl says. "Which is private *and* secret. You can't even *find* it if you just search. Anyway, good luck getting in at this point without a ticket or some serious connections." She makes a little noise in the back of her throat. "Oh, and you'd also need a car because this place is basically in the middle of nowhere." She crosses her arms and smirks.

"Well, what if we have one," Sean says. "A car, I mean. And what if we were willing to drive out there . . ."

Jamie-girl leans forward. "Well then, maybe we could work something out . . ." She's trying to sound calm but under all her eyeliner her left eyelid twitches. "Because we happen to have those very special connections one would need to get in last minute. We were planning on going but then smoochy-face's car broke down. But if you give us a ride there and throw in the picture of course, we might be . . ." She's starting to smile, but she takes a deep breath and forces the corners of her mouth down. "Well, we might be *willing* to come with you to Phoenix and help you get in and help you get backstage. We'd have to leave, like, now though."

"And we'd have to stay overnight somewhere," Jamie-boy says. "Y'know, all together." He grins. "You guys in?" He sticks his hand out to shake. He has bits of green ink on his fingers, too.

"We're in," Sean says. But when he sticks his hand out, Jamie-girl steps forward and wedges herself in between Sean and her boyfriend. "Wait! Before we agree to anything" — she glances at me and for a second almost looks embarrassed — "you guys *are* a couple, right? I mean, because otherwise, this could get . . ." — she glances at her boyfriend — ". . . awkward."

"No, we're not a couple," Sean says slowly, shaking his head. "Where did you get that idea? We're brother and sister." And then without missing a beat, Sean reaches up and puts his hand on the back of my neck. He turns and then starts gently pulling me toward him. His face is coming closer, his lips parting. I can't breathe. And then, his lips are touching mine. I close my eyes. I'm floating in space and the only parts of my body I can feel are the ones he's touching. He holds me against him for one more moment and then lets me go long before I'm ready. Jamie and Jamie stand there with their mouths wide open.

"Kidding!" Sean puts his arm around my waist and gives me a little squeeze. "Ellie's my girl. Right, El?"

And all I can do is nod because I'm too shocked to do anything else.

# EIGHTEEN

Sean and I are sitting in the car pulled up in front of the Jamies' apartment building, acting like nothing happened. Or rather, Sean is acting like nothing happened, while I am silently freaking out.

"Riding for twelve hours with the Jamies is definitely going to be funny," Sean says. He pauses. "Question is will it be the kind of funny that makes a person laugh? Or the kind that makes a person barf a little?" Sean grins. I try and laugh but it comes out sounding like a cough. I know it didn't mean anything, Sean was being resourceful, just doing what he needed to do to get the Jamies to come with us, but I can't stop thinking about the kiss. Lip against lip, his hand on the back of my neck, our bodies pressed together. I know it was only for show, and I know I don't have much experience to judge it against, but I swear, I swear, that kiss felt real.

Sean's phone starts vibrating. He takes it out, looks at it, hits *Ignore*, then shoves the phone back in his pocket.

"Oh!" I say loudly, awkwardly. "I should call Brad. At work. I'm supposed to go in tomorrow."

"Uh-huh," Sean says. "Go for it."

And as I dial Mon Coeur, Sean's phone buzzes again, he silences it without even looking. A thought I don't want in my head pops in and won't leave. What if Amanda was right? What if all those "wrong numbers" he's been getting are actually some poor girl calling to see where her boyfriend is? I shake my head. I am thinking Amanda's thoughts here. Not my own.

Brad answers on the second ring. "Bonjour, Mon Couer!"

"Hi, Braddy," I say.

"Ellie-face! Hello! So is he your boyfriend yet? Are you preggo? Are you naming the baby after me?!?"

I laugh. "Um . . ." I glance at Sean. He's staring out the window.

"Don't you 'um' me, missy. So how was the ride home? Did you invite him up? Did you smooch him?"

"It was good," I say.

"What was good? The ride *or the smooch*?!"

I don't say anything.

"Ellie . . ." Brad says slowly. "You are not answering with the candor to which I am accustomed . . . *Are you with him right now?*"

"*Yes*," I say. "I am."

"No way! What are you guys doing?"

"We're in Denver. And we're on our way to Phoenix."

Brad pauses. "Hold on," he says. "I have to go put my head back together because you just made my brain explode. Are you serious?" Brad sounds thrilled.

"Yup," I say.

"What are you doing there? *Is this your honeymoon?*"

I bite my bottom lip. I really don't like lying to Brad, but I also don't feel like I can tell him the truth. At least not all of it. At least not right now. And he sounds so excited about what he thinks is going on . . . "We're going to see a band play," I say. "This band called Monster Hands. Which is part of why I'm calling you, actually. Would it be okay if I didn't come in to work tomorrow?"

"You're calling me to say you suddenly, out of nowhere, hopped in a car with a hot stranger and now he's driving you to Phoenix to see a band and *you want to know if you can have off work?*"

"Um . . . yeah?"

Brad lets out a loud *WHOOOP*. "Well, of course you can! Hold on!" And then I hear him repeat what I told him to a guy in the background. Thomas probably. "You have to promise me one thing, Ellie-bean."

"What's that?"

"After you and that hot fellow are done sexin' it up, you will tell me all the details!"

I laugh.

"Promise me," Brad says.

"I promise!" I say.

There's a scuffling sound in the background.

"Hi, Ellie." It's Thomas. "Please excuse my el-pervo boyfriend. What he meant to say is that he is so excited for you that you are having a nice time with someone, and I cannot wait to meet this fellow you're with, and get back safe."

More scuffling.

Brad again. "And take a video!"

I'm laughing. "Bye, guys," I say. "See you when I get back."

"HAVE FUN!" they call into the phone together. And then they hang up.

"Everything cool?" Sean asks. He turns toward me and there's the slightest hint of a smirk on his face, and immediately I start blushing until I realize that he's not smirking at me, but what's behind me: Jamie-girl and Jamie-boy emerging from the front door of their building, red-faced, each hauling one end of an enormous blue duffel bag, like the kind of bag you might have if you were going on a three-month-long sea voyage for which you also needed to pack your own food. Sean leans toward me. "Which do you think is most likely to be in that bag, a month's worth of clothes? Or the chopped-up bodies of the last two people they hitched a ride with?" But before I can answer, grunting Jamies-boy-and-girl are piling their bag into Sean's open trunk and shoving themselves into the backseat.

"Seriously," Jamie-girl says, as she shuts the door behind them. "You guys are so lucky you met us. A Jamie-Jamie road trip is a special and unique thing. No one who goes on one ever forgets it."

"Well, that" — Sean turns to me and raises his eyebrows — "that I do not doubt for a second."

# NINETEEN

Six hours into the trip and the Jamies are in the backseat doing something that sounds an awful lot like sex although I'm not planning on turning around so I cannot say for sure.

All I know is that there's a rhythmic thumping against the back door; and it's growing faster. And for some reason that I do not even care to think about, the car is beginning to smell like yogurt.

Sean cracks the window and turns the music up. I stare straight ahead.

Truth is, even this might be preferable to what they were doing for the first five and a half hours of the trip, namely singing along loudly (and badly) with the Monster Hands album which they streamed through their phones, telling us a very, very, very long story about how they met, followed by them fighting about: 1) the details of their meeting (they disagreed on what Jamie-girl was wearing that night), and 2) a joke Jamie-boy made about Jamie-girl being controlling (which, while possibly true, was mean and not very funny).

I glance over at Sean again. He turns the stereo up. The

Monster Hands song "Some Things I'd Rather Not Discuss (About My Face)" is playing:

*Stop looking, stop stop looking at this, stop looking at this thing on my faaaaace. On my faaaaaa . . .*

Monster Hands is about to hit the chorus when the music stops. Just stops, completely.

And then a new noise emerges from the backseat, a little *yip yip yip* like a tiny dog yelping in pain.

*Yip yip yip. Yip yip yiiiip.*

I feel a laugh starting to bubble up.

*Yip yip yyyiiippp.*

I hold my breath and clamp my lips together, ball my hands into fists, press my nails into my palms, but the *yip-yip-yipping* is faster now, higher pitched.

*Yipyipyipyipyipyip.*

I turn toward Sean, his face a mirror of my own, lips bit, cheeks puffed out, eyes watering.

My chin is trembling with pent-up laughs and then . . .

"*Woof,*" Sean whispers. And it's all over. A laughter bomb explodes in the car. The more I hear Sean laughing, the more I laugh, and the more I laugh, the more he laughs. My stomach hurts, and there are tears trickling down my cheeks.

It's a full minute and a half before our laughter subsides, both of us gasping for hiccuppy breaths.

And then, finally, the car is quiet except for a soft shuffling and the sound of a zipper being zipped. I turn toward Sean again, and he shrugs and I shrug and then Jamie-girl says, loudly,

126

"We've been in the car for like six hours now, and it's twelve-thirty, don't you think it's about time we stopped for the night?"

And Sean says, "There's a little place about ten miles from here in New Mexico that I've been to before, we'll stop there."

And then Jamie-boy says, "Good. I could really use some sleep, I'm exhausted."

And then I look at Sean and he looks at me, and it turns out we weren't done laughing after all.

# TWENTY

Twenty minutes later we drive up in front of an enormous fancy-looking stone building. At first I think we're turning around because this couldn't possibly be the place Sean was talking about. This is the kind of hotel people stay at when they have so much money that they never have to think about the fact that money exists at all. Even Amanda's family doesn't stay in hotels like this one.

But Sean pulls all the way up to the front and stops the car where the valets are. A guy in a forest-green uniform opens the door and Sean gets out, and meanwhile more people in identical blue suits are opening the Jamies' doors and my door, too.

Sean gives the valet his keys and the valet gives him a ticket. And then the valet says he'll get someone to come out and take our bags for us and then Sean says thank you and gives the valet a ten dollar bill that he has somehow magically procured from his wallet without ever opening his wallet and the valet is all "very good, sir" and "thank you, sir" and none of them seem to think it's odd that he's calling Sean "sir" even though Sean's way younger than he is. Sean stretches his arms.

"Um . . . I think this place might be a little bit out of our price range," says Jamie-girl.

"Don't worry about it," says Sean. "My treat." He starts walking toward the hotel.

"So, what, is your boyfriend like some trust-fund baby or something?" Jamie-girl puts her hands on her hips and gives me this weird, almost *accusatory* look, and I shrug because I truly have no idea what is even going on. And we all follow Sean through the tall oak doors.

The moment we're inside, three of our jaws drop, literally drop like we're in a cartoon. This is, without question, the fanciest room I have ever been in in my life: There are pure white marble floors flecked with gold, floor-to-ceiling windows draped in yards and yards of cream-colored silk, an arched ceiling rising four stories overhead, and what must be the world's largest crystal chandelier dangling in the center of the room like a glittering planet.

"And you're paying for this for real? Like with money?" Jamie-boy asks slowly. "We're not going to have to jump out the windows in the morning or sneak out in the laundry hamper or some crap?"

Sean laughs and shakes his head. "Don't worry about it, dude," he says. "Seriously. I've got it." And with that Sean heads up to the counter and starts talking to the woman at check-in. A minute later, I walk up behind him as she's saying, "And so the rate for each room will be six hundred fifty for the night, plus tax." Sean must not have realized how much this was going to cost when he offered to pay for all of it. I mean, obviously he hadn't. I try and calculate how many days of working at Mon Coeur it takes me to earn this much money, how many days it probably takes my mother working at the hospital. I put my hand on his back. "Hey, we can totally . . ." I say quietly.

But Sean nods casually and hands the woman a black and gold credit card and a moment later, she gives him the two sets of room keys. Two bellhops come to lead the four of us up to our rooms. Jamie and Jamie are completely silent in the elevator, exchanging these glances like they think they've just won the lottery.

"See you guys tomorrow," Sean says. A second later we walk into the room and Sean gives the bellhop a couple folded bills. And then a second after that the bellhop's shutting the door behind him with the faintest of clicks.

# TWENTY-ONE

And then we're alone.

"I hope you're not too disappointed that I put our Jamies in a separate room," Sean says. "I thought perhaps they needed some private time." Sean grins.

I grin back. "I think they already had their *private* time in the car," I say.

"Well, maybe *we* needed some private time," Sean says. He's joking but I feel my face getting hot.

I look around the room, which is at least as big as the entire top floor of our condo, and probably bigger. It's decorated in chocolate browns, crisp whites, and deep reds. There's a seating area off to one side: a wood-and-glass coffee table surrounded by an enormous brown leather couch. In the center of the table is a thick glass bowl filled with perfect-looking dark red apples. There's a giant TV mounted on one wall, and across from it is an enormous king-size bed covered in a pristine-looking white duvet and about fifty dark red pillows. The air smells faintly of honey.

"Since it was so last minute, they didn't have any rooms with two beds. Sorry about that. I'll crash on the couch."

And I just nod. An image of Sean and me in that bed together tries to work itself into my brain but I do not let it. There's a little basket on top of each nightstand filled with beautiful things — a silk eye pillow, lavender-scented pillow spray, a little vial of something, a little jar of something else, and on top of it a card on thick card stock: *With our compliments.*

"This place is amazing," I say. I hold the eye pillow up against my cheek. The fabric is cool and smooth.

"Yeah, it's nice. Sometimes these places can be a little ridiculous." He grabs an apple from the bowl, wipes it off on his shirt, and takes a bite.

"We didn't have to stay somewhere like this, though."

"I know," Sean says. "But it's fun, right? I mean, I love me a crappy motel as much as the next guy, but sometimes you need to go deluxe."

"But it's crazy expensive . . ."

"Oh." Sean waves his hand in front of his face. "*That* you don't need to worry about. Like at all. My family is . . . comfortable." He looks up at me and shrugs.

"How comfortable exactly?" I clamp my hand over my mouth. "Sorry, I take it back. That was rude."

Sean laughs. "You can ask me anything you want."

"Okay, then I take back my taking back. How rich are we talking here?"

"Let's just say I once stayed in a hotel like this for six weeks straight, and I doubt my father ever even noticed when he got the bill."

"Damn." I say. "I guess that answers my question."

"Yeah," Sean half smiles. "It's not even my dad's money. It's my mom's money, but she's not around, so I feel it's like my duty to spend it before the stepjerk does."

"Oh God," I say. "Your mom . . ."

"No, no, not dead." Sean shakes his head quickly. "She lives in a 'therapeutic living community,' which is basically the rich-person's version of a mental hospital slash rehab facility."

"Why is she in there?"

"Because she enjoys their healthful 'spa cuisine' . . . well, that and she's a completely crazy drug addict slash alcoholic slash who-even-knows-what."

"Do you miss her?"

"I miss the *idea* of her," Sean says. "Y'know, the idea of a mom. But I don't remember her well enough to miss the actual her. She went there for a 'break' when I was about six, and then never came back. Less than a year after that, my stepmom and my stepbrother moved in. My stepbrother is the one who . . . y'know. Anyway, even though he's remarried now, my father still has power of attorney over her because she's been deemed 'unfit,' which basically means he can spend as much of her money as he wants."

"Wow," I say.

"Yeah," Sean says. "All I need is an evil identical twin to come and toss me down a well and my family could star on a soap opera." He walks over to the shiny mahogany desk. "But what are you gonna do? It's why I don't feel bad spending the money."

"Do you ever see her?"

"Not really," Sean says. "I went to visit her once when I was seven, the Thanksgiving after she left. It was too weird, though. She didn't recognize me at first because they had her on so many drugs, which is ironic, considering." He finishes the apple and tosses the core across the room into a black wood trash bin where it lands with a *thunk*.

"That's horrible."

"It is what it is, I guess." Sean shakes his head and smiles. "Sorry, I don't mean to be a downer. I don't usually talk about this stuff to anyone, I just feel like I can with you, I guess, which is kind of a relief."

"You can," I say. And I feel a squeezing in my chest. I'm grateful to be the listener for once, to be able to be there for someone else. "You can talk to me about anything."

Sean sits down on the leather couch and looks up at me, "Well, let's talk about room service then. I don't know about you, but spending a bunch of hours in the car listening to strangers have sex always puts me in the mood for cheeseburgers and champagne."

"Funny," I say. "I was thinking the exact same thing."

A little while later a man comes in pushing a rolling silver cart bearing two cheeseburgers, an oversized bottle of champagne in a silver bucket, and a giant slice of chocolate cake. He opens the champagne and pours two glasses. Then he looks at Sean's black Converse and his floppy skater hair, at my cutoff shorts and tank top, and shakes his head slightly. Sean signs the bill. The man leaves and Sean and I are alone again.

We sit on opposite ends of the couch and Sean hands me a glass.

"To being understood," Sean says. We clink and there's a little fluttering in my stomach. I've only had champagne once before, at Amanda's house, when her parents had a party and Eric stole a bottle for us. Eric and Amanda drank most of it.

This champagne is cold and delicious. A second later, my glass is empty. Sean's is, too. "Glasses are for babies," he says. He picks up the bottle and takes a long swig. Then hands it over to me.

"Actually, I think babies mostly drink out of bottles," I say. "Well, and boobs, I guess." I think the champagne has already gone to my head. Sean laughs. I take a gulp and pass it back to him. And we do this for a while; pass the bottle back and forth, back and forth.

And now the bottle is almost empty and Sean is leaning back against the couch and staring at me. Just staring so intently.

"What?" I say. I raise my hand to my face.

Sean reaches out and moves it gently away. "I'm just looking at you," he says. And his voice sounds so sweet. I close my eyes for a second and think how even though there are hard things and scary things in the world, there are also really nice things, like sitting across from a guy you're maybe really starting to like. A guy who maybe, just maybe, is starting to like you, too. I wonder what it would be like to have Sean as a boyfriend, I wonder what it would be like if . . .

Suddenly, a thought uncurls itself from the back of my brain. And the champagne has dissolved my filter, so I just open my mouth and say it. "Do you have a girlfriend?"

"What made you ask that?" He lowers the bottle. "Wait, is

135

this because of what Amanda was saying on the phone earlier? I wondered when you were going to bring that up."

"Oh God," I say. "You could hear her?"

"Your speaker volume is up really high," he says. But he's smiling.

"I'm so, so sorry. Amanda's just . . ."

"Don't even worry about it, seriously." He waves his hand. "Stories tend to get screwed up when they get passed from person to person, and I don't care what those people think, anyway. The short version is that no, I do not have a girlfriend. There was a girl and I loved her and I knew she loved me, but things were really complicated and we couldn't be together. I tried to fix it so that we could be, but it didn't work out." Sean looks away. "I think when you find someone you really care about, you have to do everything you can, y'know? Because all that corny stuff about how love is the only thing that really matters is . . . well it's true. Only sometimes love makes people do crazy things. And sometimes, no matter what you do, a relationship can't happen. Especially when one of the people in it isn't even trying."

For a moment he looks so very sad. Without even thinking about it, I reach out and put my hand on his knee.

"Whoever she was, she made a mistake."

He shakes his head. "You're a sweetie," he says. And our eyes meet and I feel myself blushing, and wonder if it was weird that I just put my hand on his knee like that, so I take it away and grab one of the forks that came with our food, and stick it into the slice of cake.

A low hum starts coming from across the room, my phone is vibrating again.

"Wait a second," I say. Something else has just occurred to me. Something even worse. "Does that mean you've heard other conversations, too?" My arm is frozen out in front of me, a bite of cake balanced on top of the silver tines. "Like maybe ones I had with Brad?"

"Um . . ." Sean says. "Kinda?" And then he waggles his eyebrows.

I think about Brad's jokes about Sean and me, the fact that I made the trip sound like a romantic date, the fact that I agreed to tell him everything . . . I feel the panic chemicals welling up in me and it's possible I am actually about to burst into panic flames.

"I was just trying to be nice to him!" I say. My entire body is sweating. "I didn't want Brad to have to worry about me! And I would definitely never . . ." But before I can say anything more Sean says, "Sssshhhh," and reaches up and closes his hand over mine. I'm still holding the fork. He's leaning forward, his arm resting on the back of the couch behind me. His mouth is getting closer. His lips look so soft. Is he going to kiss me? He is absolutely definitely going to kiss me.

I tip my head to the side. I close my eyes, I part my lips.

And wait.

And wait.

"Dude," Sean says. I open my eyes. He's nodding his head and pointing to his mouth. "Now *that* is some Goddamn good cake."

I look at my fork. It's empty.

"Your face is red," Sean says. "Are you okay?"

My champagne buzz is completely gone.

"Oh, did you think I was about to . . ." Sean says. He points back and forth between our mouths.

I shake my head. I am outside of my body now, dead from embarrassment. I'm going to go into the bathroom now and see if I can flush myself directly down the toilet.

I start to stand. But Sean has wrapped his fingers around my wrist again. "Ellie, don't go," he says. And he's pulling me toward him slowly. And I do not have any cake on my fork this time. And I do not remember anything else terrible. I close my eyes.

# TWENTY-TWO

I wake up and the events of last night come back in flashes, the way dreams do:

Lip against lip, mouths opening. Time slowing down, speeding up, slowing down. We are on the couch. We are on the bed. We are on the floor. We are magnets. We are melting. We are ordering more champagne. We are drinking from each other's mouths. We are drinking from each other's skin. We are breathing heavy. We are *yip yip yipping*. We are cracking up. We are playing strip poker with fries as cards. We are winning. We are losing. We are naked. We are covered in sweat. We are licking it off. We are pressed together. We are going faster. We aren't stopping. *We are going too fast*. We are slowing down. We are curling ourselves together into a ball. We are comparing our scars: white lines on my shin from slipping on wet rocks, tiny white circle of an ancient chicken pockmark on my hip, scratches on his arms from a lifetime of dogs, scraped up knees from falling off a bike, that tangle of jagged white lines on the inside of his arm for reasons he can't say. We are breathing together. We are heartbeating together. We are starting all over again. We are not sure where his body stops and mine begins. We are drifting off into something like sleep.

I lie here now, on this beautiful bed in this beautiful hotel room. Silk eye pillow wrapped around my wrist like a bracelet. My head pressed against the pillow, my face stuck in a smile. I reach out for Sean. But the bed is empty. I'm alone.

Alone?

I sit up. There's a glass of water next to the bed. I don't know how it got there. I pick it up and drain it. My head aches, like my skull is slightly too small to hold my brain. My tongue feels fuzzy. My lips are sore. I get out of bed. I am naked except for one sock. I pull the sheet off the bed and wrap it around myself.

"Hello?" I say. My voice isn't working right. "Sean?" My whole body feels fragile, like I'm made of glass. I make my way around the room, sheet dragging behind me. Every bit of evidence from the night before has been cleared away. No champagne bottles, no room service cart. Even the balled-up napkins we used in the napkin war have magically disappeared.

My phone is on the table. It's flashing. I have two text messages: *stop ignoring me*, from Amanda, and also *I'm worried about you*. And four missed calls. All from her. But nothing from Sean. And I realize I can't call him, because I do not even know his number.

I walk to the enormous bathroom. The door's halfway open. No Sean.

I lean against the wall.

What if last night didn't really happen the way I'm remembering it? What if I changed it around in my head to be what I wanted?

A new picture starts to present itself. Me, drunk and embarrassing myself. Sean kissing me because he felt sorry for me. Me talking too much. Laughing too loud. Annoying poor Sean who just wanted to eat some dinner and go to sleep.

I go into the bathroom and look at myself in the giant mirror over the sink. There are bags under my eyes and my hair is sticking out in all directions, there are pillow creases on my face and dried drool on my cheek. I turn the shower on steaming hot. I get in and let the water run over me. There are a half dozen tiny bottles lined up along the tub. I close my eyes and tip my head back. I scrub my hair with basil mint shampoo. Wash myself with sea salt shower gel. I dry off and wrap myself in a thick white towel. I brush my teeth, hard.

I open the bathroom door and watch the steam escape. I pad out into the bedroom, I smell food and before I even realize what it is, my stomach is grumbling.

"Bacon, egg, and cheese?" Sean's back, sitting on the couch, a brown paper bag clutched in his hand. He's staring into it.

"Oh hi," I say. My heart thumps painfully in my chest. I'm very aware that I'm not dressed.

"When you're hungover, you need grease," he says, matter-of-factly. He still doesn't look up. "Scientists have done science studies about it." He pulls out two tinfoil-wrapped sandwiches. "I found a diner a couple miles away. The Jamies are still sleeping,

I think." He tosses one sandwich toward me, barely glancing in my direction. I reach out awkwardly. The egg and cheese falls to the floor at my feet. "We should hurry up," he says. "Get on the road as soon as possible." There's no warmth in his voice. He is all business now. "It's already past noon and we have about six hours more driving to do."

"Okay thanks," I say. "I'm going to get dressed now. Then I'll be ready to go."

Sean still hasn't looked at me. He nods to his sandwich and takes a bite.

*This is worse than I thought.*

# TWENTY-THREE

The four of us are in the car again.

"Do you want me to turn the air down?" Sean asks. He doesn't look at me.

"That's okay," I say.

"What?"

"This is fine."

"Okay," Sean says.

"Okay," I say. "Thanks for asking."

"No problem," says Sean. This is how it's been since he came back with the sandwiches, like we suddenly don't know how to talk to each other anymore.

"Look how polite they are!" Jamie-girl says. "He treats her like a *lady*. Why don't *you* ever treat me like a lady?"

"Well, maybe I'll treat you like a lady when you start acting like one," Jamie-boy says. In the rearview mirror I see him grab her boob. She lets out a squeal and a laugh.

Moments from last night flash through my mind: Sean stroking my hair. Sean kissing my neck. Sean's hands on my . . . I turn toward him, but he's watching the road. And if he notices me in his peripheral vision, he doesn't let on. A wave of loneliness sucks at my insides. I think back to Saturday afternoon when he showed up at the store, and Friday when he was staring at me at the party. We feel more like strangers now than we did the very first time we met.

I bet Nina never had a morning after like this. It's probably part of what made her so attractive to people — she was always comfortable, always at ease, always knew what to do next. I want to say *Why can't we be normal to each other?* I want to say *Don't you like me anymore?* But instead all I do is force a cough, because this is the most appropriate conversation starter I can think of.

"You okay?" Sean says.

"Yeah, I had a tickle in my throat."

Pause.

"I hate that," he says.

Pause.

"Me, too," I say.

Then silence again.

If we actually do find Nina, I'll definitely need to ask her what the hell a person is supposed to say in a situation like this. But for now, I just lean my head against the window and stare out.

I try to convince myself not to care — whatever happened last night doesn't matter. Whatever happens with Sean doesn't matter. None of this matters.

Now if only I could get myself to believe it.

# TWENTY-FOUR

It's like another planet out here — massive green tubes topped with spiky red and yellow balls sit next to cabbage-size flowers with inch-thick petals, and delicate ten-foot stalks curve their graceful limbs up toward the sky. The sun is setting now, in swirls of pink and orange and purple, the colors so bright it seems impossible. My brain has decided we're no longer on earth, a fact it supports with the strange plants, the hair-dryer hot air, and the red mountains off in the distance. This is, I guess, why people travel in the first place. Surrounded by all this, I am having trouble holding on to my own sadness. It no longer seems to make sense. Nothing does.

It is hours later and we are in the desert in Arizona.

"Two more miles on this road," Jamie-boy says. "And then one more left and then it should be right there on our right."

We keep driving and a few minutes later, we see a couple dozen people lined up near the side of the road, next to a long line of cars pulled off onto the shoulder.

"Looks like this must be it," Sean says.

Jamie-girl claps her hands together. "Yeee!"

Sean parks and we all get out. The Jamies are dragging their giant duffel bag behind them.

"You can leave that in the car," Sean says. "I mean, you don't want to carry it around for the whole show do you?"

"Ah," Jamie-boy says. "But we do!" He bends down and unzips the bag halfway and removes two black T-shirts. He hands one to Jamie-girl and pulls the other on over his head. *Monster Hands Monstrosity Tour Staff* is silk-screened in green on the back.

"Okay, so they're not the most *professional* T-shirts, but they get the job done," Jamie-girl says, winking. "We make them ourselves, you know!"

Jamie-boy hoists the bag back up onto his shoulder and pats it affectionately.

"Thanks for the ride, guys," Jamie-girl says. She pulls a little square of fabric from her pocket and pins it to the side of the bag. *Official Monster Hands Merch* it reads in the same green ink. "And for the hotel room and everything. Good luck!" They turn to go.

"But wait!" I say. I hear the panic rising in my voice. "What about how you said you'd help us get into the concert? And meet the band?"

"Oh, yeah, that," Jamie-girl says. She frowns for a second. "Well, I mean, you'll be fine. The ticket line's right there. It's not like the show's sold-out or something. I mean, Spit Pavilion is really big." She shrugs. "As for meeting the guys, well, you're on your own with that one, sweetie. We've been trying for forever and the closest we've ever gotten is the time their manager kicked us out of their show for selling unofficial merchandise." Then she grins. "Anyway, we gotta run, this bag o' Monsty isn't going to sell itself! Oh, and don't worry about us getting back, we'll figure it out. As you might have noticed, we're really quite resourceful!" Jamie-boy gives me a final up-down look and then the two of them walk off, calling, "Official Monster Hands T-shirts, thirty-five dollars! Official posters of the new Monster Hands album cover, twenty dollars! Monster Hands monster hands, forty dollars! Official bottles of Monster Hands monster water, seven dollars!"

And Sean and I are both left standing there in the warm Arizona sunset, watching them go.

"Whoa," Sean says. "What just happened there?" But he's more talking to himself than to me.

We join the line, behind a girl in black flip-flops, a denim miniskirt, and a gray T-shirt with the neck cut out that keeps drifting over one smooth shoulder. She has a pair of large gray rubber hands strapped over her real ones like gloves.

"I have no idea," I say. "Really no idea at all." The girl in front of us turns around. She's beautiful — heart-shaped face, huge eyes, long dark hair.

"You know those guys?" she asks. She points with one of her giant monster fingers to where Jamie and Jamie are working their way down the line.

"Not really," Sean says. "Although we did spend the last like thirty-six hours with them."

"Oh my, my, my," the girl glances at me, then back at Sean,

then glances at me again. She's trying to figure out if I'm his girlfriend. "Ah yes, the Creepy-Jamies, infamous in the Monsty scene for being super shady and also . . . being rather, um, *open* about their private activities. Did you happen to notice that during your thirty-six hours of Jamie?"

Sean nods. "We may have been treated to some triple-X live Jamie-on-Jamie action."

The girl puts one of her giant monster hands on his shoulder. "Oh, you poor dears," she says. But she's looking only at him now.

A hot prickle of jealousy creeps up the back of my neck. A warm wind blows and ruffles her silky hair.

"So where are you guys from?" the girl asks.

"Awfully far away," Sean says.

"You must be a very loyal fan," the girl says, "to go through all that."

"Something like that," says Sean.

"Loyalty's important," says the girl.

They continue talking as we work our way up to the front of the line. I feel like I'm not even there. And in this moment I wish I wasn't.

Fifteen minutes pass and we're only a few feet away from the doorway now. The girl flashes her ID and heads inside. And that's when I spot a big sign *21+ for entry. No ID, No Entry, No exceptions!* I nudge Sean, who takes something out of his wallet and shows it to the bouncer. A fake ID. And now it's my turn and I'm paralyzed. "Come on, Nina," Sean says. I turn toward him. He nods. "You have your passport, don't you?" Of course. The passport. I take it out and hand it to the bouncer who barely glances at it before stamping the inside of my wrist with the face of a tiny monster and ushering me inside.

Spit Pavilion is one giant room with scuffed wood floors and super high industrial-looking ceilings. There's a stage straight back and a bar off to the left with dozens of people crowded in front of it and hung up behind the bar is a giant white-horned animal skull, the kind of thing you'd see tied to the front of a truck, except this one is way too massive to be real. The place smells like a mix of beer and wood smoke. I glance at Sean. His hands are in his pockets and he's looking around, maybe trying to find the monster hands girl? I force myself to turn away and remind myself why I'm here.

An opening band is playing: two guys on drums and a girl in lederhosen singing:

*Nein nein nein! No no no! Nein nein nein I'll see you in the snow!*

And then, finally, the lederhosen girl stops singing, and a guy in a bright red suit comes onstage and takes the mic.

"That was Lady Bratvoorst direct from Germantown, Maryland. Give it up for Lady Bratvoorst everyone!" The crowd lets out a weak cheer. "And now, the Spit Pavilion could not be more thrilled to bring back one of our very favorite bands of all time. We love them. You love them. *Your momma loved them last night*. Put your gray rubber hands together for Monster Hands!" The crowd goes insane, screaming, making loud monster growls while the three guys from the photo I stole run out onto the stage.

A moment later the music starts and all around me, people start dancing. I feel something inside me beginning to lift.

And then I feel something cold and wet splashing on my leg.

"Oh no! I'm very sorry!" I turn to my right, there's a great big guy about one-and-a-half times the size of a regular person, wearing a pair of giant rubber monster hands, standing there shaking his head. "Gravity!" he calls out. "It's particularly strong over here I think!" I look down, there's an empty beer glass tipped over on its side, pouring out around my flip-flops. "And these hands are really hard to hold stuff with."

"It's okay," I call back.

"No one likes beer-feet! Let me get something to dry you off at least." The guy takes one of my hands in his monster hand and drags me toward the bar. I turn back to look at Sean, but the spot he was in seconds ago is now empty.

The guy grabs a stack of napkins off the bar and hands them to me. "Lest you think I am not a gentleman, I will not attempt to dry you. I'm Danny by the way."

I bend over and dry myself off, and when I stand back up, Danny is still there.

"I swear I didn't spill on you on purpose just so I'd get to talk to you," Danny says. "But if I'd seen you before I spilled . . . I might have!"

"Thanks?" I say. "I think?" Danny's grin is big and goofy, more funny than flirty. I crane my neck looking for Sean again. Where *is* he?

"Shall we dance?" Danny says. He sticks out his hand.

I keep looking around. No Sean. I feel a stab of disappointment. But no. I shake my head. And I remind myself that this trip
is not about Sean. And whatever happened between him and me
doesn't matter. We were drunk, and it's not like he's my boyfriend
or something. If Sean wants to go off and do whatever else with
whoever, well that is his business and no concern of mine . . . right?

For the next hour, Danny and I dance like crazy — arms up,
hips shaking, bouncing to the beat until we are drenched in sweat.
The hangover sadness is lifting, and whenever I start to think
about Sean, about last night, or about the weirdness today, I dance
harder, dance sillier. And by the time Monster Hands plays the
final chord of their encore, "Big Sneaks Sneaking," I am feeling
kind of okay.

I excuse myself when the song is over. It's time to do what I
came here to do.

There's a shiny black door next to the stage blocked by a giant
guy with waist-length curly hair and a giant brown leather jacket. I
watch as two girls in tiny matching gray dresses approach the door.
They're saying something to the guy. He's shaking his head. They're
pouting. He crosses his arms. One of the girls pulls down the front
of her dress and shakes her boobs at him. He doesn't seem to care.
The girls give up, give the guy the finger, and slink away.

I take a deep breath. And as I walk, I try and channel my inner
Nina. The big guy with the curly hair is holding the door open
while another guy comes through carrying a giant amp. I look the
big guy straight in the eye and smile my biggest, Nina-est smile.

"I'm here to see Monster Hands," I say.

The guy just stares at me.

"I'm not some random fan, we're friends."

"Sure you are, honey." He shakes his head and lets go of the door.

"I'm serious!" I say. "They'll be really happy I'm here!"

"Listen, I'll tell you the same thing I told those ladies over there." He motions toward the girls in the gray dresses who are now at the bar doing shots. "The boys in the band didn't tell me about any special guests tonight, and until I hear it from them, you're not getting backstage. I've been with them on this entire tour, and when someone's coming for a visit, they let me know."

"Well, I'm here to surprise them! Tell them Nina Wrigley is here and see what they say."

"Your name means nothing to me and I'm not going to bother them, they like to relax after a show."

And suddenly something occurs to me. "I drew the art for their most recent album cover. You know that drawing with the girl screaming with her head tipped back?"

"Yeah . . ."

"Well I did that," I say. I fish the drawing from Attic out of my pocket and show it to him. "Here's another piece I did. A self-portrait." He stares at it. He's considering this. "And I'm the one who tattooed Ian's stomach."

"Alright, alright, I'll go and ask them."

The guy disappears behind the heavy metal door and reappears a few minutes later, looking embarrassed.

"I'm so sorry about that, Nina. We've had a string of crazy fans trying to get back lately so I've had to be kind of a jerk about it. They're really excited you're here, they said to send you in. Go all the way back."

And then he winks and steps aside. And now I'm heading down a crowded hallway lined with guitars and amps, and a dozen or so people are hanging out drinking beers. A guy in a charcoal gray suit is standing in front of a doorway at the end of the hall yelling "this is not a negotiable issue" over and over into his phone, emphasizing different words each time. "This is *not* a negotiable *issue, this* is not a *negotiable* issue." I walk past him and through the door.

It's strangely quiet, as though all the noise of the hallway died at the entrance. The two red-haired guys are sitting cross-legged eating bowls of cereal, one on the couch and one on the floor. The black-haired guy is standing by an open window, shirtless in a pair of pajama pants with kittens printed on them. They all look up when I walk in.

"Who the feck are you?" Kitten Pajamas asks in a thick Irish accent. He's smiling. I recognize him from the picture; he's the one who had his arm around Nina.

"You're not Nina," says the guy on the couch. He sounds very disappointed. "Where's Nina?"

"You here for some cereal?" asks the guy on the floor. He has a short red beard, and a tiny milk mustache. "We've got Cinnamon Toast Crunch and Froot Loops. I myself am partial to a mix of the two."

"Don't offer her cereal," says Kitten Pajamas. "She lied to big Jimmy. She's a Nina impersonator! She could be a crazed fan here to kill us!"

"We're not famous enough yet for that, Ian," says the guy on the floor.

"Like hell we're not! So, I would like to restate my previous question, who the feck are you?"

"I'm Ellie Wrigley," I say. "Nina is my sister."

Ian/Kitten Pajamas narrows his eyes. I hold out her passport. He takes it, looks at the picture then holds it out toward the guy on the couch. "Peter, check this out."

Peter takes the passport. "Well would you look at that." He shakes his head.

"You okay there?" Milk Mustache asks. He wipes the mustache off his face.

"So you guys did know her then," I say. "And you knew her pretty well?"

"Not as well as he would have liked," says Ian.

"I knew her," Peter says. "A bit." He looks up at me. There's tension around his eyes, like he's in pain but trying not to show it. "How's she doing?"

"I'm not sure," I say. "I haven't seen her in a very long time. She disappeared two years ago."

"We kind of figured something was up with that girl," Ian says. "Why'd she go?"

"Don't know that, either," I say. "I'm trying to find her. And I saw a photograph of you all with her at Bijoux Ink in Denver, or, well, I stole it actually. And then I saw a drawing she did that someone told me is going to be on your new album."

"And whoever told you that?" Ian asks. But he looks amused, not annoyed.

"A really big fan of yours," I say. "Well, two actually. Both named Jamie."

And Ian shakes his head. "Ah, the mad gingers."

I nod.

"Well, that's not a surprise, I don't suppose, although I have a hard time imagining you associating with the likes of them. Then again, now what's this you said about stealing from Bijoux?"

"Um." Perhaps I shouldn't have mentioned this part, but it's too late now. "The woman who worked there said she didn't even know Nina, but I could tell that she did and then I got into the back room and when I saw the picture of you guys with my sister . . . I hid it under my shirt and snuck out."

Ian looks at me, and then at his bandmates, and they all burst out laughing. "Good on ya then," Ian says. "God love her, but Eden deserves something like that now and again. Ah, Bijoux," Ian shakes his head. "Favorite tattoo place in our old hometown, well, our second hometown after our first one. Bijoux is the site of my greatest shame." He stands up. "I bet Peter and Marc here I could toss eight balled-up napkins in the trash without missing one. I was sure I could do it!" He pulls his kitten pajamas down slightly; there on his stomach is the tattoo from the photo — Marc's and Peter's faces, inked in black. "Turns out I couldn't."

"Now whenever a young lady so happens to be spending time

down there," Marc/Milk Mustache, grins, "she's staring me and Peter in the face."

"So far I haven't had any complaints," Ian says.

"Well why would you?" Marc lifts his cereal bowl to his lips and drains the last of the milk. "We're gorgeous."

Ian adjusts his pajama pants. "If I won, they were going to have to get my face on their arses."

"You should consider yourself lucky to have that," Peter says, and then turns to me. "Your sister was a genius. A true artist."

"Nina was only in Denver for a couple of weeks," Marc says. "But poor Peter fell in love with her straight away. Wrote a song about her and everything, but never had the guts to tell the girl."

"He's shy," says Ian.

"We were younger then and he didn't yet realize that being a big famous rock star means if you like a girl, chances are she'll like you back," Marc says.

"That's enough, boys," Peter says, shaking his head. "She just wasn't interested, alright? Nina wasn't the type of girl to care about fame or any of that crap." He looks down at his lap. It's sort of insane to think that this is the same guy who was doing hand-stands on stage only a few minutes ago.

"I think she had a boyfriend," I say. "I thought maybe she left with him."

"Well, not when we knew her she didn't." Ian says. "Or if she did, he certainly wasn't with her when she left with us."

"What do you mean?"

"She hitched a ride with us out of Denver. Poor Peter was so

156

excited when she asked if she could come." Ian sits down cross-legged on the floor, staring at the kittens dancing on his knees. "She was only with us for a few days, though. She left us when we got to Big Sur."

"Why there?" I ask.

"Dunno," Ian shakes his head. "She had us drive her up to this big house. She said she had to say good-bye to someone there, but we never found out who or why. And then that was it. My last memory of her was her standing in front of this giant house holding her little overnight bag and this snowboard, waving."

"Why did she have a snowboard?" Something clicks in my head. The other charge on her credit card bill was from Edgebridge Sports. I'd almost forgotten.

"To go snowboarding, I assumed." Ian shrugs. "She was a mystery, your sister. And not too fond of questions. We asked her to stay in touch but she never did. She left that drawing behind though, the one on our new album cover."

Peter stands up and walks over to a purple chrome case. He opens it and pulls out a record album. He hands it to me. "This is an advance copy." Nina's drawing is on the cover. "She never even got to see the album," Peter says. "Never even knew that we put her drawing on there, actually. Will you take this and give it to her when you find her?"

"Of course," I say. And hearing him phrase it like that, *when*, not *if*, *when*, makes me smile. "Is there anything else you can tell me? Anything she might have said about what she was doing or where she was going or . . . anything?"

"Well, like I said, we dropped her off at a big house in Big Sur," Ian says. "I bet you Peter remembers. He made us go back a couple months later on the way back to Denver."

"It was on our way," Peter says. "Sort of . . ." Peter picks a green notebook up off the floor and pulls a pen out of the spine. He tears out a little sheet of paper and scribbles on it. "There," he says, handing it to me. "That's the address. Don't know how much good that'll do you though. When we went back the place was all deserted-like except for this lonely seeming groundskeeper fella who was wandering around trimming the hedges. Said no one had been there in months."

"It's worth a try at least," I say.

"*Do* you want some cereal?" Marc has stood up and is pouring himself a bowl. "I feel like we know you well enough now . . ."

I smile. "I should go back out there." I motion toward the door. "But thank you."

"She was a lovely girl, your sister was," Peter says. "When you see her, would you give her this, too, for me?" Peter scribbles something else on a piece of paper and hands it to me, looking ever so slightly embarrassed. It's his phone number.

"I will," I say.

"And if you're in a pinch," Ian calls out after me, "you could always sell that album on eBay!"

# TWENTY-FIVE

I'm back out in the main room of Spit Pavilion, there's soft music playing over the sound system, and no one is dancing. And I am wandering through the quickly thinning crowd looking for Sean. I let the questions swirl through my head as I go. If Nina was alone by the time she met Monster Hands, then where was J? Did they run away together and then break up? And why didn't she come back after that? Or did they break up and then get back together? Is she living with him somewhere?

And also, *Where's Sean?*

I look back at the stage. Just off to the side, a couple is pressed against the wall, limbs entwined. The guy has short dark hair and a dark T-shirt, jeans. Just like Sean. The girl's hair is long and dark. My stomach burns with hot liquid jealousy. The guy turns his head to the side, as though he can feel me staring at him. Not Sean. I feel a flood of relief.

"Ellie?" I hear someone calling my name. *Amanda?* "Oh my God, Ellie! *There* you are!"

I turn and Amanda wraps me in a hug. Then she leans back,

159

lets out an excited little "aah!" and then hugs me again. "I got here a little late and I was worried maybe you'd *left!*"

The sound of her words and the motion of her mouth seem slightly out of sync, like she's been badly dubbed.

"Ellie?" Amanda leans back again and looks at me. "Hello?"

I'm not sure what to say. I'm too confused to say anything.

"Aren't you happy to see me?" But I can't answer because I honestly don't know.

"I went to Mon Coeur yesterday and Brad said that you were going to see this band in Arizona, and I thought, wouldn't it be so fun if I surprised you? I mean, it's summer, we both know it's not like I do that much at Attic, anyway. So I decided what the hell! Why not get a plane ticket, right?" She throws her arms up over her head. "So, SURPRISE!!!!"

She lowers her arms and then claps her hands together. It's like she's trying to rewrite a story that we were both part of and thinks I won't notice that she changed it. As though it will somehow erase the weirdness of the last few days.

But before I have a chance to decide whether I want to express any of this, I feel a warm hand on my arm.

I turn. Sean.

"There you are." His voice is soft and low. A hint of a smile plays on his lips. This is the Sean I remember from last night. The one I have been missing all day.

"Are you going to introduce us, Ellie?" Amanda puts her hand on her hip. She's trying to sound perky, but her voice has an edge.

Sean looks at me. Our eyes meet. I feel that jolt of connection. I take a deep breath.

"Sean, this is Amanda." Surprise flashes across his face and his jaw tenses.

"Amanda, this is Sean." I try and imagine what she sees — dark hair that's flopping in his face, black T-shirt, smooth jaw. Does he look the same to her as he does to me? A moment from last night pops into my head — his smile when we pulled away from a kiss, the glint in his eye as we caught our breaths.

He's watching me still. I feel my face getting hot.

"Hey, Sean," Amanda says. "Nice to meet you."

"Hi, Amanda," he says. But he's still staring at me.

I want to tell him about everything that happened backstage, but I can't do that in front of Amanda. Not anymore.

Amanda glances down on the floor, in front of her is her big cherry-print overnight bag. She's wearing a pair of high-heeled strappy leather sandals. Her toenails are painted bright pink. It's as though she dressed up special for this.

"Amanda came to surprise me," I say to Sean. "Brad told her I was here seeing a band."

Sean doesn't say anything.

"So where are you guys staying?" Amanda says.

Sean reaches out and puts his hand on my lower back. "We don't know yet." I feel the heat of him soaking through my shirt. "We were going to find a place after this."

Amanda glances down at Sean's arm. A look of deep discomfort flashes across her face, as though she is suddenly realizing what she's gotten herself into. And what a bad idea this might be. For a second I feel sorry for her.

"This'll be fun," Amanda says, but it sounds so forced, not one of us believes her.

# TWENTY-SIX

In a parallel universe, Ellie2 is in a hotel suite in the middle of downtown Phoenix, with her best friend and the guy she likes, having so much fun! They're laughing and joking around. They're having a dance-off and ordering cake from room service! When Ellie2 leaves the room to go to the bathroom, she overhears them talking about how great she is, how much they love her, how they want to plan a surprise party for her together. When she gets back from the bathroom, they all jump on the bed and take hilarious pictures to add to the photo collage they're making to document this, the greatest night of their lives!!!!

But in the regular universe, the one I happen to live in and the only one I know about, things are going rather differently. Well, the beginning is the same: I am in a room at the Golden Oasis Suites in Phoenix with my best friend and the guy I like, but there's been no laughing, no cake, no dance-off. The only surprise party we're having is one where we are all surprised to know it's even *possible* for things to be this awkward. And it's sure as hell no party.

We checked in thirty awful minutes ago, and now at this moment Sean is sitting on one of the queen beds, looking desperately uncomfortable, flipping through channels on the TV. Amanda is standing by the door of the suite with her hand on her hip and a towel over her shoulder, frowning. And I am in between the two of them, with no idea what to do next.

"Hello? Ellie? Are you coming?" Amanda wants to go swimming. She lives for pools. Ordinarily she can be rather particular about things, but she'd swim in a dirty puddle if someone put a sign that said *Pool* in front of it. And there happens to be one here at the hotel, on the roof, and it's open all night.

"I don't have a bathing suit," I say. "How about you just go without me?"

Sean settles on a documentary about elephants.

"I brought an extra one," she says. "The navy blue boy shorts one that you wore at my house that first night it got warm back in May. Remember, Eric's friend Dylan kept watching your ass all night?" She goes to her cherry-print bag and pulls it out.

I glance at Sean who is leaning back now, watching a big elephant help a little elephant climb out of a hole. He scratches his stomach through his shirt. The blood rushes to my face. I remember how it felt last night when we were pressed together, belly to belly, my cheek on his chest, his hand in my hair. Was that really just last night? Amanda crosses her arms.

"Are you sure you don't want to come?" I ask Sean.

"Nah, I'm tired." Sean shakes his head. "I think I'm gonna hang out here with my buddies." He motions to the elephants.

"Here," Amanda says. She sticks her hand out, the navy blue straps dangling from her fist. "Go into the bathroom and change."

And even though I don't want to, I'm at a loss for how to fix any of this. So I do what I'm told.

Suits and towels on, Amanda and I head out into the beige and cream–colored hallway. The second the door clicks shut behind us she turns to face me. "What the hell is going on?"

"With what?" I ask. Even though I'm pretty sure I know.

"Um, I don't know, how about with you randomly disappearing on some road trip without even telling anyone first? And then avoiding my calls? And then playing boyfriend/girlfriend with that guy back there? I mean, I know things were a little weird the last couple times we talked to each other, but just because we get into a fight doesn't mean you have to run off with some creepy loser."

"Stop it," I say, "you don't know him." We walk toward the elevator. I push *Up*. About a second later the gold-and-glass elevator arrives and we get in.

"Neither do you," she says. Amanda presses the button for the roof. The elevator begins to rise. The doors open and we step out into a lush desert oasis — there are dozens of multicolored cactuses in terra-cotta planters, a half-dozen wood patio tables shaded by dark green umbrellas, and four cream-colored canvas cabanas draped in hundreds of twinkling white lights, all surrounding a crystal blue swimming pool that's lit from underneath.

I turn to my right where Amanda was standing, but all that's left of her is a pair of flip-flops and a towel in a pile on the ground.

I hear a splash and watch concentric circles spread themselves out over the surface of the pool. Amanda's wet head pops up in the center of it. Even though it's after midnight, it's still at least ninety-five degrees out. I dip my toe in; the water is pleasantly cool. I close my eyes and jump.

The pool lights glow gold through my eyelids as I sink down to the bottom. It's so quiet down here, so peaceful. I stay until my lungs are burning. When I reach the surface, Amanda's right there in front of me.

"Okay, all I want to know is this." Her face is lit from underneath, all lines and sharp angles. "Since when do you go off on vacation with random guys like a day after meeting them?"

"We're not on vacation," I say simply. And as soon as the words leave my lips I regret them.

"So then what are you doing here?"

I pause and take a deep breath.

"We're looking for Nina," I say.

Amanda stares at me. I hear sounds, people moving around near the edge of the water, but the lights in the pool make it hard to see outside of it. I swim to the ladder. Amanda doesn't follow.

"I don't even know what to say to you," she says. She sounds so disappointed.

"I didn't ask you to say anything."

"I'm worried about you," she says. "I cannot watch you do this to yourself anymore. I mean I came all the way out here to make sure you're okay . . ."

"And what *exactly* are you worried about?" I say. "That I'm actually going to find Nina? That someone else is helping me who isn't you?" Even *I* am shocked to hear myself say this. But the words are out now. And I can't take them back.

"No, Ellie, what I'm worried about is that you've lost touch with reality and you somehow think driving hundreds and hundreds of miles with someone you don't even know is a perfectly normal thing to do."

"Who cares if it's normal?!"

Amanda swims over to my side of the pool.

"Do you really think it's a good idea to be here with that Sean guy? I mean, what do you even know about him? What is he even doing here?"

"He wants to help me," I say. "And at this point he is the only person in my life who is willing to."

"Are you sure about that?" says Amanda.

"About what?"

"Are you sure that his intentions are really so pure?"

"What else would he be here to do?"

"I think all he wants to *help you* with is taking your pants off."

"That's not true!" I shake my head. I don't want to be here in the water anymore. I climb the ladder, and wrap myself in my towel. I feel Amanda watching me. I turn around.

"Helen's nephew said he was a total stalker!" Amanda's arms are crossed over the side of the pool.

"I don't give a crap what Helen's nephew thinks."

A hot wind blows. Goose bumps rise on my wet skin. I wrap the towel tighter.

"So what happened *exactly*? You met him at the party and you told him you don't know where your sister is and he was like, 'Great, okay, girl who I met three minutes ago, I'm going to volunteer to drive you across the country with no ulterior motive whatsoever?' I mean, who does that?"

"Someone who understands," I say.

"Oh, so he 'understands' you? And how is that exactly?"

"Because he's just like me!" I'm yelling now.

"You're nothing like him!" She's yelling, too. "He's a freak!"

"No," I say. "He's not. Or if he is, then I am, too. He gets what it's like for me, with Nina, in a way no one else does."

"And what makes him so special?"

"His brother is dead," I say. I'm speaking softly now but my tone is ice. "That's why he's here and that's why he's helping me. Because he understands what it's like when someone is there one day and the next day they're not. And how that's not something you can *get over*. So if you think he's weird or you think he's a freak, it's only because *you* don't understand. And lucky for you that you've never had to."

For a moment, there is silence.

"And you believe him?" she asks. I can't make out Amanda's expression with her back to the light. But she doesn't sound even the slightest bit sorry.

"What?!"

"How do you even know he's telling the truth? How do you know this isn't some dramatic story he made up to get close to you and to get you to go on this insane road trip with him? Let me ask you a question, did he tell you about his dead brother before or after you told him about your sister?"

I don't say anything.

"And what did he tell you this brother of his died of?"

"I didn't ask!" I don't know why I'm even still answering her.

"Well, I bet he made it all up," she says. "I bet he never even had a brother."

"Shut up!" I shout. "Shut up. Shut up. Shut up. SHUT UP!!" And when I stop, she is quiet. I hear footsteps, someone running toward the elevator. I turn and there's Sean. He's pressing the button, the doors are opening, he's stepping inside. "Sean!" I call out. He turns and a look of pure anguish passes across his face as the doors close. He's gone.

I run toward the elevator.

"Wait!" Amanda calls out. "Ellie!" I keep going.

There is a stairwell next to the elevator. I push through the door and start running down the stairs, two at a time. I hear Amanda behind me. Down, down, down we go. Thirteen stories later, we tumble out into the hallway, panting. The door to our room is cracked open. We enter.

Sean is crouched on the floor, leaning over his black leather bag, his back to us.

He closes the bag and clicks the lock shut. He stands up slowly. He's holding something in his hand. He walks over to the desk near the doorway and places a square of newsprint on top of it. Then he steps back.

"I would never lie to Ellie." He doesn't sound angry, just very sad and very, very tired. "Go ahead and read it."

Amanda picks up the newspaper article and I read the headline over her shoulder.

"Elm Falls Teen Dies of Drug Overdose."

*Early Thursday afternoon, one day after celebrating his 18ᵗʰ birthday, Jason Cullen was found dead in the home of his mother and stepfather in Elm Falls, Illinois, by his stepbrother Sean, 14.*

I hear Amanda's sharp intake of breath. Tears spring to my eyes. *Memorial services were held late Friday at Our Lady of Grace, in West Edgebridge. "He was the kindest person I've ever known," said Max Davies, 20. "My family moved around a lot my entire life, Tennessee, Florida, Pennsylvania, but Chicago was the first time I actually felt at home. And that was because of Jason. He was my first friend and my best friend. The fact that he's no longer alive isn't going to change that." His family could not be reached for comment. Authorities have yet to determine whether the overdose was accidental or suicide.*

To the right of the article there's a picture of Jason, grinning in a graduation hat. Strong jaw, wide mouth. He looks happy. I feel like I've seen him somewhere before. He has that kind of face.

Sean is by the desk, looking down. I go over and put my hand on his back.

"Well, so now you know," he says. And he smiles this small sad smile. And without meaning to, I can't help but picture it — fourteen-year-old Sean walking into his brother's room to say good morning, to see if his brother wants some breakfast. Jason is lying in his bed, maybe Sean thinks he's asleep. Maybe he always sleeps late and this is a familiar scene, or maybe he usually gets up early and the fact that he's not up yet is already odd. He's lying in bed. Is he dressed? Is he wearing pajamas? Maybe Sean says good morning, calls him a dickhead or a snotwad or whatever it is brothers call each other. Sean waits for his brother's response, but it doesn't come. Maybe Sean thinks this is a joke at first, or maybe he thinks his brother is just sleeping extra heavily. Sean calls his name again. His brother still doesn't answer. Sean tries again. And again. Exactly how many times does Sean call his brother's name before he realizes something is wrong? Does he shake him? Does he check his breathing and take his pulse? Does he run out of the room? Does he scream? Call 911? Does he still have hope or did he know right away? And how does he live with a memory like that floating in his head, polluting and darkening all the others?

I turn to Amanda, who has the strangest look on her face. Maybe it's shame. Maybe it's horror. I don't know. I don't care.

"I think you should go now," I say to her.

Amanda reaches out and tries to take my hand. I pull away.

If it is time to pick sides, I am choosing. I have chosen. I lean against Sean, wrap my arms around him. Amanda looks up, her mouth opens. "Just go," I say. My voice is cold, hard. Amanda flinches. Things will not be the same after this.

# TWENTY-SEVEN

The moment Amanda is gone, everything changes. It's like she took all the bad air in the room, packed it into her cherry-print overnight bag, and took it downstairs with her to catch a cab to the airport. And now, Sean and I can finally breathe again.

We turn toward each other. "Sean, listen . . ." I start. I am about to apologize for what happened, for everything Amanda said, but Sean just shakes his head. He has a sweet dreamy smile on his lips. He pulls he toward him. "Thank you," he says. "Thank you." He holds my head against his chest and whispers into my hair. "Thank you, thank you, thank you, thank you." And although I'm not even entirely sure what he's thanking me for, I nod and hug him back. His T-shirt is warm against my skin.

He puts one hand on the side of my neck and brings my face toward his, brushing his lips so gently against my cheek I can barely feel them. He kisses me again, right next to my mouth, again on my chin, my forehead, the tip of my nose, again and again all over my face. When he finally presses his lips to mine, my insides turn to liquid. "Come," he says, and leads me toward the bed. He lies down and pulls me on top of him, arranging my body like a doll's, my head on his chest, my arms around his neck.

"This is fate, Ellie," Sean whispers.

I know there are things I need to tell him, about meeting Monster Hands, what they said about Nina, about the house in Big Sur, and I know I need to call Brad, and maybe my mom, too, but when I look up and see Sean's face, so close to my own, I decide all that other stuff can wait. For the first time in a long time, I'm happy exactly where I am and I'm exactly where I know I need to be.

# TWENTY-EIGHT

At some point during the night, I am jolted awake by motion and noise. Sean kicks at the blankets, his arms are around my shoulders, tightening, releasing, his fingers are scratching at my back. He's sweating, his skin hot against mine. Animal cries escape through his clenched teeth.

"Sean," I whisper, and then louder. "Sean!"

He's trying to say something, but the words come out garbled. "Indint safe-im, Indint safe-im."

"You're having a nightmare," I say. I wrap my arms around him. "Everything is okay. You're having a nightmare." He puts his arms around my waist and clings to me, his head against my chest. I move slightly to adjust the pillow under my head. "Mmmmmm," Sean says. And he shakes his head, like "don't go away," like "stay here with me." Like he's scared I'm going to leave. I stroke his hair. "I'm not going anywhere," I say. And I lie there with my arms around him. I lie there like that until the cool blue light of morning starts coming through the window. And only then do I finally fall back asleep.

# TWENTY-NINE

I wake up with sunlight streaming into my eyes, my cheek crushed against Sean's chest. When I lift my head, he smiles, and he kisses me on the lips. "Morning, baby," he says. "You're an awfully gorgeous thing to wake up to." And he kisses me again.

"Well hello there," I say. My mouth is dry. I start to get up out of bed.

"Awwww." Sean pulls me down on top of him. "Not yet." He gives me a squeeze. A rush of warmth courses through me.

I lean back against him. "Those were some crazy nightmares you were having last night."

"Nightmares?" Sean looks confused. "I was?"

"Yeah," I say. "What were you dreaming about?"

Sean frowns. "Don't remember. And it doesn't matter anymore, anyway." He is pulling me toward him again. My phone buzzes on the nightstand. I grab it and glance at the screen. The caller ID says *Mon Coeur*.

It's 11:17. I was supposed to be at work over two hours ago. Hundreds of miles away. I pick up.

"Braddy! Oh my goodness, I am *so sorry*." But I am smiling

because I know as soon I tell him about me and Sean, he'll be so excited for me, he won't even care.

"Hey, Ellie," Brad says. He doesn't sound terribly happy.

"I completely forgot to call you!" I say. "I'm so sorry. I should have asked for today off, too. I somehow didn't think of it when I was talking to you on Sunday." I untangle myself from Sean and begin to stand up. He grabs my wrist. I blow him a kiss, and then pull away and walk toward the bathroom. "But you won't be mad when you hear where I am! I'm in a hotel room with . . ."

"I know," Brad says.

"You do?" I glance at myself in the mirror. I try and smooth down my hair.

"I saw Amanda." Brad's voice sounds strained. "She came by on her way home from the airport."

"Oh?" I freeze. My phone beeps, I glance at it. The red battery icon is flashing.

Brad doesn't say anything for a minute.

"Braddy, whatever Amanda said isn't true. And she was a real bitch."

"Friend," Brad's voice softens. "You know I love you, but Amanda sort of freaked me out a little bit this morning when she was here. She was really worried about you."

"She's not really worried, she's jealous," I say.

Brad sighs.

"What did she say?" I ask.

"That the guy you're with might be . . . a little weird."

"Amanda thinks *everyone* is weird!"

"Well, you have a point there." He pauses. "When are you coming back?"

I think about the address Peter gave me that's still in my pocket, and I think about Sean back in the bed. "In a few days?"

"Okay *fine*," Brad says. He's trying to sound begrudging, but I can tell from his voice that he's happy for me. And that is why I love him. He *wants* to be happy for other people. Unlike Amanda, who just wants to be controlling.

"Thank you, oh Braddiest," I say. And then I pause. "I think he could be my Thomas."

"Well, I think I will have to be the judge of that!" Brad says. "Bring him in to meet me *for real* and then we'll talk."

"Okay!" I say. I rinse my mouth out and then start walking out of the bathroom. The battery beeps again. "Shoot, my phone is out of batteries. I don't have my charger with me so it's going to cut off soon."

"Okay," Brad says. "I expect stories when you get back. Kissies!"

"Kissies!" I hang up and wander back into the main room.

Sean is still in bed. "Hey, who are you giving kissies to that isn't me?!"

"Brad, from work," I say.

"Well, don't use up any kissies on him that are rightfully mine!"

"Hey, would it be okay if I used your phone for a second? I'm out of batteries and I should call my mom, I guess." She works the overnight shift on Mondays, and today is Tuesday, which means

177

she'll have turned her phone off and will be sleeping. Which is the perfect time to call.

He curls his finger, beckoning me over, then taps his cheek. I give him a peck. "That's more like it." He hands me his phone. I scroll through my contacts, find my mom's number, and dial it into his phone right before my own powers down.

It goes straight to voicemail: "Hello, you have reached Jane Wrigley. I'm unavailable at the moment, leave a message and I will call you back as soon as I am able." I can hear the stress in my mother's voice, the lack of joy. It somehow seems even more obvious now than it used to, maybe because I haven't heard it in a while. Maybe because I'm suddenly so happy myself.

"Hi, Mom," I say. "Wanted to let you know I've been at Amanda's house these last few days, which you probably assumed. And I'm still here. Anyway, okay. Hope work was okay. Bye!" I hang up. A tiny part of me feels the tiniest bit guilty for lying, but what's the alternative?

Sean reaches up and grabs me around the waist, pulls me down into bed with him.

"I was supposed to work this morning. And I totally forgot," I say.

"Oh, what a terrible shame," he says. He nuzzles my neck.

"It's okay, though, Brad's not upset." I sit up.

"That's good," says Sean. "But, y'know, you don't have to have a job anymore if you don't want to."

"What do you mean?"

"Well, as you know, I have plenty of money, and I hope this

offer won't make you feel weird or anything." Sean blushes. "But you could just have some."

I'm blushing, too. "That's really sweet," I say. "But I'd . . ."

"Wait, wait, wait," Sean says. "Get that *no* look off your face. I'm only saying that if we decide we don't want to come back for a while, if we want to go on a road trip somewhere else, maybe drive over to my family's vacation house and relax there for a bit, you shouldn't feel like we can't because you have to go back to work, that's all." Sean smiles again. "Maybe we *should* go to the vacation house. It's really beautiful up there and I haven't actually been in like two years. Or we could go visit, I don't know, anyone. We could pick some random person online and then ask them, 'Hey, can we come over for dinner?' and then we can drive to wherever they are. We can bring a pie! Or we could go to the Grand Canyon. Have you ever seen it? Not just a big hole in the ground! Makes a person feel tiny in the best way possible."

I smile back. "That all sounds really wonderful . . . but there are some things we haven't even talked about yet."

"Oh!" Sean says. "Of course. I should have brought it up already, I'm really sorry about that."

"Oh, totally, don't worry about it."

"No, I mean it, I'm sorry. I swear I wasn't hitting on her, things were so awkward between you and me then and I wasn't sure what you were thinking and I didn't want to pressure you about anything. I was just trying to be friendly to that girl, but I can see how that would have been weird for you. If it'd been the other way around, I would have been so jealous. And don't worry, I'm not mad about that dude."

"What dude?"

"The one you were dancing with last night," Sean says. "None of that matters now. It feels like so long ago, anyway."

"I was talking about Nina," I say. "And me meeting Monster Hands and the stuff they told me."

"Oh," Sean says. "Right, of course." He shakes his head. "Tell me."

I repeat the story and show him the album. "And Peter wrote down the address of that house they dropped her off at." I take the slip of paper from my pocket and hand it to him.

"Thirteen seventy-two Ledgeview Pass, Big Sur, California," he says very slowly, very deliberately. "This is where they dropped her off?" He sits down on the bed, his back to me. He coughs. The tips of his ears are turning red.

"Yeah," I say. "So I guess that's the next stop!"

Sean coughs again. "I don't know." He shakes his head. "Didn't you say Monster Hands already looked for her there?"

"Yeah, they did. I figured it'd be worth the trip to check the place out anyway, because it obviously meant something to her, and she definitely went there once . . . like all the other places we've been going to." I'm suddenly very confused.

Sean takes a deep breath. "Are you *sure* you want to? Like, are you sure you want to keep going like this?"

"I don't know what you mean."

"Well, I've been thinking about it, and I wonder if *this*" — he moves his hands back and forth between us — "is the reason you found that drawing of Nina's. Not so you could find Nina, but so we could find each other." He puts a warm hand on my arm, and looks me straight in the eye. I feel that flash again, the one I felt when I first met him. Only now for some reason it makes me nervous.

"But what about what we talked about?" I say. "About how it's impossible to get over a thing like this? About how . . ." I stop. My face grows hot. What's going on here? I turn away.

"Oh no." Sean's voice softens. "I'm sorry. I'm sorry, Ellie." Sean sighs and shakes his head. "I'm not trying to keep you from searching for her. Forget what I said, okay? We'll go to Big Sur and look for her." He wraps his arms around my waist. "We'll leave right now, okay?" He squeezes me tight. I can feel his heart pounding hard through his shirt. This is Sean, sweet, wonderful Sean.

I nod, and then I smile as relief washes over me. "You'll love her," I say. "When you meet her, you'll really love her."

But Sean doesn't even smile back this time. He steadies my face with his hands and stares at me. "I couldn't love anyone else now," Sean says. "Because I already love you."

# THIRTY

According to the clock, we've been driving for an hour, but it feels like it could have been a minute or a week or a year. Time doesn't matter anymore.

And for that matter, neither do words. We're immersed in silence, not the cold jagged silence of yesterday, but a different kind, like warm liquid. Everything we need to say we communicate through our hands clasped together between the seats, through the tiny gentle motions of finger against finger, palm against palm.

And all I can think is *This is it, this is what it's like to be falling in love.*

Sean pulls off at an exit for a rest stop. "We need snacks," he says. "And gas, too." He drives for another minute and then parks. He stares out the front window, and I try to interpret his expression. Does he look a little anxious? I squeeze his hand. "I'm going to run in here," he says. He unplugs his phone from the car charger, squeezes my hand back, and gets out.

I lean back and watch him cross the parking lot. I love the way he walks, shoulders squared, head hanging down ever so slightly. I put my bare feet up against the dash, and the cool air blows against my legs. Over the soft hum of the air conditioner I hear the muted blend of sounds from outside. Laughter and shouts and cries and car horns. Sean disappears into the building.

A minute passes, and then another one. I feel a gnawing in my stomach and I realize something so silly it makes me laugh out loud — I miss him. Sean has been in the rest stop for all of four minutes and I *miss* him. I will tell him this when he gets back. He will love this. He will laugh, too!

And then we will drive to Big Sur where I very well might, no, scratch that, where I *will* find a clue that will finally lead me to Nina. And then my life will be perfect. Then my life will be absolutely complete.

I watch the door. Four guys emerge with McDonald's bags. A father with a screaming kid is coming out with a ketchup-stained shirt and a pile of napkins. And then there's Sean walking through the door; he's so beautiful. I remember when I first saw him, back at the Mothership. Back then, if someone had told me what he would end up meaning to me only four days later, I never would have believed it. How could I have? How could I have even begun to understand?

As he gets closer, I feel myself smile. I start to wave, but he just stares at me through the window. He has the strangest expression on his face.

He comes over to my side of the car, opens the door, leans in, and wraps his arms around me.

"I was just thinking about how I missed . . ." I start to say.

"Oh, Ellie." He leans back. Takes both of my hands in his. He raises them to his lips and kisses them one by one. He looks like he's about to cry. Adrenaline is rushing up and down my spine.

"I have to tell you something," he says.

An awful thought flashes through my mind — maybe Amanda was right. Maybe he has a girlfriend after all. I turn away. "Ellie, please look at me," he says. "Please."

I look him straight in the eye.

"My family knows this private investigator, okay? My father hired him for something once, a few years ago, something for his company." He pauses. Takes a deep breath. "This guy is pretty much the very best there is. He's an ex-FBI agent and has contacts everywhere. If a person exists on this earth, he can find them."

"Okay . . ."

"So when I first met you and found out about Nina, I thought, maybe I was meant to meet you to help you with this, to help you find her. I called him when we stopped at that first rest stop on the way to Nebraska."

I nod.

"I didn't want to get your hopes up in case he didn't find anything, so that's why I didn't mention it before."

I nod again.

"Anyway, yesterday when we were at the show, when you were dancing with that guy, I went outside and called him to check in . . . he had some information."

My heart is pounding. It's pounding so hard and loud that I can barely hear Sean anymore.

"This morning, when I was saying how I thought maybe we should stop looking . . . I" — Sean swallows — "it's because I had talked to him before and the stuff he said did not sound good and . . ."

"Did he find her?" I hear my voice ask. I sound so quiet, like I'm far, far away from myself.

"Ellie," Sean says. He takes a breath. Then opens his mouth again, and his lips are moving, but the weird thing is now I can't hear anything at all. It's like the world has gone silent. He's motioning with his hands. He's nodding. But *I don't hear anything*, except for the beating in my chest, like someone pounding on a drum. Sean takes me by the shoulders. I hear a gurgling, like water rushing past my head. And then *whoosh* the sound comes back, loud, too loud. Cars honking. People laughing. "Ellie did you hear me?"

"I'm sorry, missed all of that," I say to Sean. And I smile. Because it is awfully strange to suddenly go deaf in the middle of a parking lot. So strange it's funny, really. "What?"

"That investigator found out some terrible news about Nina," Sean says. "I'm so, so, so sorry." Sean looks like he's going to cry now. "She died." Sean looks at me again. "Ellie, Nina is dead."

And I nod. Because turns out I guess I did hear him after all. But I can't think about any of this right now because someone is screaming, a high-pitched, blood-curdling, ragged shriek of a scream. It's so loud that everyone turns in the direction of it. And it makes it hard to think, all that screaming. And then I realize something: It's not just someone screaming. It's me.

# THIRTY-ONE

I remember one night when I was seven, lying in my bed, listening to my parents fight. They'd been fighting a lot back then, but this time was different somehow. It was so loud that I could even make out actual words: my father yelling that he was leaving, and my mom yelling that he should stop threatening and just get the hell out already. A few days later, my father *would* leave, but I didn't know that yet. All I knew was they sounded so angry, so out of control. And I was so scared.

My bedroom door creaked open and Nina crept in. I remember the way she looked, standing there in her pajamas, backlit by my nightlight. Without saying anything, she led me out into the dark hallway, then into the bathroom and shut the door behind us. She flipped on the lights. I saw then that she was wearing her fluffy orange earmuffs, and she was holding my green ones. She put them over my ears and then she turned on the shower but we could still hear them over the rush of the water. So she began to sing:

*HAPPY BIRTHDAY TO YOU,*
*HAPPY BIRTHDAY TO YOU*

It was late September and my birthday wasn't for months, but Nina had always said "Happy Birthday" was the very greatest song in the world because after you heard it, there was usually cake.

*HAPPY BIRTHDAY, DEAR BELLY . . .*

*HAPPY BIRTHDAY TO YOU*

When we finished, she waggled her eyebrows and then started again.

*HAPPY BIRTHDAY TO YOU*

*HAPPY BIRTHDAY TO YOU*

*HAPPY BIRTHDAY, DEAR BELLY*

*HAPPY BIRTHDAY TO YOUUUUUUU*

By the time I joined in, I was smiling, too, and the world was beginning to make sense again.

*HAPPY BIRTHDAY TO YOU*

*HAPPY BIRTHDAY TOOO YOOOOOOOUUUU*

So my parents were crazy and hated each other. So what? It didn't matter because I had Nina. And whatever happened, she would take care of it. She would make the world fun and silly and safe. Like she always did.

*HAPPY BIRTHDAY, DEAR NIIIIIIINAAAAAAAAAA*

*HAPPY BIRTHDAY TOOO YOOUUUUUUU*

After what felt like the millionth verse, we stopped to catch our breath. The fight was over, the screaming had ended. Nina opened the bathroom door a crack to make sure. The cool air rushed in and steam escaped into the dark silent hallway.

But Nina looked at me then and shrugged. She closed the door back up. We kept on singing.

# THIRTY-TWO

I am outside of my body now, watching as Ellie, who has just found out her sister is not alive anymore, sits up and wipes the vomit off her chin.

This is how Ellie reacts when she finds out her sister is dead: She screams for a while and then she barfs on the pavement.

Ellie wants to ask questions, but it is hard at this particular moment for her to remember what words are and how to form them. She closes her eyes until eventually one drips down from her brain and pops out her mouth.

"How?" Is this the word she meant?

Sean reaches out and puts his hands on Ellie's shoulders. She can't even feel it. "Are you sure you want to hear this right now?"

Ellie's voice says, "Yes."

"She was killed," Sean says. And then he winces, as though wincing for Ellie who is sitting there perfectly still. "She was living in Las Vegas and working in a club as — " Sean looks hesitant " — as a stripper. She started dating a guy who was a big poker player. He was known for making really insane bets. Sometimes he'd win a couple hundred thousand dollars in a night. And other times he'd lose it. He had a losing streak once, a serious one. And he borrowed money from some really bad people and then he couldn't pay it back. And one night the guy he borrowed money from was beating him up, really badly, out in the parking lot of the club where Nina worked. He'd come to pick her up and the guys he owed money to found him there. Nina was upset. She got involved. There were guns. And . . ." Sean pauses again, as though he's scared to tell the end of the story, as though if he doesn't say it, it won't have really happened. He takes a deep breath. ". . . She got shot and then that was it."

Sean's mouth twists itself into a grimace of pain. He probably feels worse than Ellie does, because, actually, she doesn't feel much of anything at all. It sounds like she is hearing about characters in a story, a story that has nothing whatsoever to do with her. She knows she is supposed to feel something now, or supposed to do something now, ask something else maybe?

"Oh," she says. And she sits there, unsure whether she is frozen in one moment or if time is still passing. "When?" Ellie asks. "How long ago?"

"Just over a year ago," says Sean.

"I need to talk to the investigator," Ellie says calmly. "Can you call him back please?"

Ellie waits as he dials. After a few seconds Sean shakes his head. "Voice mail," Sean says. "He told me he was on assignment when I talked to him, so he's probably not able to answer his phone." And then back into the phone he says, "Hey, Doug, this is Sean Lerner calling again. We spoke before, but I need to ask you some more questions, please give me a call back." And then he hangs up and looks at Ellie. "We'll try him again later, if he doesn't call back in a couple of hours."

Ellie nods, as though she understands. But here's the most perplexing part: For an entire year Ellie has been living on a planet that her sister is not a part of, for an entire year, and somehow *Ellie didn't even know.* Ellie stares out the window at the people in the parking lot, walking places, holding things, talking to one another. All those people have managed to survive all the many different things in the world that could kill a person, all the different times they were in danger, all the different times they could have died, they didn't.

And Nina did.

I pop back into my body then, and I remember: *The world doesn't make any sense at all.* People tell you it does, try and pretend it does. But I know what kind of place this is, what kind of world we live in. And my breath catches in my throat, and my heart rips apart not just for me, not just for Nina, but for all of us.

# THIRTY-THREE

And it doesn't take long for me to remember how to cry. I lean over in the front seat, my arm against the dashboard, my head against my arm, the sobs coming out of me as though all the holes in my face lead to an endless supply of tears. Then the memories come, like a photo slide show with my crying as the soundtrack:

Nina blowing up a hundred balloons and filling my room for my ninth birthday. Nina drawing a cartoon about my socks and leaving it in my sock drawer as though my socks drew it themselves. Nina driving us to 7-Eleven the day after she got her license, flirting with a guy in the parking lot until he bought me a Slurpee and her a six-pack of Amstel. Nina sneaking back in at five in the morning in a pink fuzzy dress, a mischievous smile on her face, putting her finger to her lips and winking as she slipped back into her room.

But then the other images come, too, invading my brain, without warning or permission. Nina running out into the parking lot of some strip club, a jacket on over high heels and fishnets. Her boyfriend lying on the ground, a large hulk of a man over him, kicking him. Nina taking a leap, flying through the air onto his back. The large man stumbling forward, then backward. Shaking her off him. Her falling to the ground. And then what? I squeeze my eyes shut. I do not want to think about these things. I can't stop myself. Does she see the gun? Is she scared? Does he hold it over her and pause, make her apologize before he shoots? Or is it a surprise, a single bullet in the back of her head, the hot pain searing through her with no warning, her dying thought a question: What the *hell* was *that*?

The tears come harder now.

We are driving again. It's later. I'm not sure what time it is. Or where we are exactly. But what does it matter? Whatever time it is, wherever I am, this will be the truth. I cannot escape from it. I will never be able to.

I cry for a while more and then I pass into a weird place of calm, an empty bubble of blank space in between all these tears, and lift my head up. In front of us is the highway. This is what the highway looks like after I know my sister is dead. This is what it feels like to sit in the car after. This is what it feels like to breathe after.

I turn toward Sean, he's chewing his bottom lip, like he wants to say something but isn't sure he should. "What is it?" I ask.

Sean takes a breath. "Do you wish I hadn't told you? I thought about not . . . I thought maybe if I convinced you to give up look-ing . . ." Sean pauses. "Would it be better if you didn't know?"

But now that I know, it's hard to even imagine what it was like when I didn't. This morning was a thousand years ago. I feel sorry for that poor innocent Ellie of earlier today, who so naively believed there was hope, that everything was going to be fine. That it ever could be.

I shake my head. "The only way it would be better is if it hadn't happened," I say. And hearing myself say these words, the crying starts again.

Sean reaches out and squeezes my knee. "I've been through this," Sean says. "I will go through this with you, Ellie. You won't be alone. I promise."

And I nod, grateful at least for that.

# THIRTY-FOUR

We're at a motel now, the Grand Sunset Lodge, a group of wood buildings surrounding a parking lot. It's not fancy or touristy; it's the type of place people go to sink into anonymity, the type of place people go to hide.

I am sitting on a bed, legs bare on the scratchy comforter, leaning against a chipped plywood headboard. I am having another one of those strange blank moments. My head feels like it's stuffed with thick cotton that somehow cushions my brain from all my thoughts.

"Are you hungry?" Sean asks. He is next to me, holding my limp hand, looking at me with such concern. I am grateful to him for being here, for expecting nothing from me. But I don't have the energy to express this right now.

I shake my head.

"If I get you something, will you eat it? I think I saw a pizza place near here. Maybe they deliver?" He pats his pockets looking for his phone. "Or we could get a bunch of snacks from the vending machines."

And now I am crying.

"What am I supposed to *do* now?" I ask.

"You don't need to think about that," Sean says. "I'll do all the thinking for both of us. I will take care of you."

And I lean back against the pillow. I reach for my phone then remember.

"My battery died," I say. And I feel the tears slipping down my cheeks now. "I can't call anyone, because I don't even know anyone's number."

"You don't need to call anyone," Sean says. "You don't need to tell anyone."

And I want to believe him, but I know that no matter how long I wait, at some point I will have to be the one to call my mother and tell her. And Amanda, I will have to tell her. And Brad. And . . . I am crying harder now. How can I exist in a world that I know Nina is not in? And do I even want to?

Sean puts his arms around me and pulls me toward him, pressing my face against his chest.

"We don't have to go back," Sean whispers. "We don't have to ever go back."

All I can do is nod. I feel the tears soaking through his shirt, spreading out until my entire face is wet with them.

# THIRTY-FIVE

Sean is in bed asleep, cheeks flushed, smiling slightly. And I am awake watching him.

I do not think I will ever sleep again. The limp wet sadness of earlier is gone, having been replaced by a hard nugget lodged in my center, its sharp jagged edges piercing my insides, filling me with a thousand questions. Who was the man that killed her? And where is he now? Is he alive? Is he in jail? And what about this boyfriend, this boyfriend she died for? Where is he? And who is he? And what about Nina? Did someone have to go identify her at the hospital? And why didn't anyone ever call my mom? And where is her body buried?

*Her body.* Her body that she is no longer in. Her body that is just meat now.

This thought fills me with such horror I raise my hand to my lips. Then lower it. The faint outline of a monster face remains on the inside of my wrist — the stamp from the Monster Hands show. I think about the album they gave me. It's in the car, with Nina's drawing. I want to see it.

I pad softly on the water-stained carpet. Sean's jeans are neatly folded and lying on top of the dresser. I reach into his pocket and get his keys. I wrap my fist around them to keep them from jingling. I glance at Sean one last time, and slip out.

I make my way across the empty parking lot, unlock Sean's car door and climb in. The album is in between the seats, on the cup holder. I tear off the plastic and take out the record. Something flutters to the floor. The lyrics printed on a delicate sheet of rice paper in dark gray ink. I read the first song.

*"Wherever Nina Lies"*
*Her face changes when she thinks you can't see her.*
*Staring out the window, always watching, someone's*
    *chasing her.*
*She twists her hands, draws pictures on her wrist, bites*
    *her lips.*
*Ask a question, she just shakes her head, won't answer it.*
*She cries at night, always cries at night, she thinks you can't*
    *hear it.*
*Try and tell her it's okay, but you know she can't believe it.*
*Ask her why and she only shakes her head no.*
*She says one day she'll go as far as she can go.*
*She says one day she'll go as far as she can go.*

And I gasp, because I understand what this last line means, in a way that whoever wrote it surely didn't. Because I know where she was planning on going now, even if she never got there: When Nina was fifteen and I was eleven, we got kind of obsessed with the weird local commercials that would come on TV late, late at night. Sometimes when our mom was working the overnight shift, we'd stay up until one, two, three in the morning waiting to see them. We loved the ad for Hammer Jones's Hardware featuring "Hammer Jones himself," and a spot for a local hair salon showing a woman with a bunch of foil on her head whom we recognized as the cashier at the drugstore. But our very favorite was the one for Covered Wagon Shipping in which a trucker dressed in colonial clothing said, "Whatever you need shipped, I'll personally drive it myself, from just across the street" — flash to him driving the truck across a street — "to clear across the country. *That's as far as you can go!*" Flash to him driving past a piece of poster board onto which someone had written, *Welcome to San Francisco* in orange marker. Nina and I absolutely loved this commercial and it became a long-running joke for us. For years all one of us had to do was say, "I'm going about as far as you can go!" and the other one would crack up.

I can imagine the guys from Monster Hands asking Nina where she was headed and Nina reciting this line. Maybe laughing a little to herself. Maybe thinking of me while she did. I smile, for a second, just for a second. But figuring out the song lyrics is not a triumph now. This is not the next clue. This is not anything.

I look back at the motel. All the windows are dark. It is so quiet out here. I feel like I am the only person in the world.

But the silence is interrupted by a buzzing coming from under one of the car seats. I lean over. There's a lit screen. Sean's phone. I reach down. *Unavailable* is blinking on the screen. It's 3:16 a.m.

I am suddenly filled with such deep anger at whoever is calling, for calling now, for being alive when Nina isn't. I answer the phone.

"She gave you a fake number," I say. "Whoever you think you are calling, this is not them. This is SEAN'S PHONE," I say. "Sean. A boy." I pause. "You do not know him!" My heart is pounding. No answer. "Hello?" I hear breathing . . . and then a voice, barely louder than a whisper.

"Get away from him, it's not safe for you there."

My stomach twists. This is obviously a wrong number, some stupid kid playing a prank probably. Or maybe Amanda is somehow involved in this. My pulse races.

"Who are you?" I say. But they've already hung up. I don't want to be in this parking lot anymore in the dark. I put the phone down on the seat next to me. I don't want to touch it. I want to go back inside the motel.

There's a tapping on the window. I turn. A hand. Big eyes. A face. There is a face, someone watching me. I open my mouth and scream.

The door opens and a pair of strong arms wrap around me.

"Hey, hey, hey, hey, it's okay, baby. It's me. It's just me." Sean rocks me back and forth. "I woke up and you weren't there."

"I couldn't sleep," I say.

"What are you doing out here?" he asks.

"I wanted to see that Monster Hands record," I say. "I wanted to see Nina's drawing . . ."

"Oh, baby." Sean's sweet face is creased with concern. He shakes his head.

"But you don't understand," I say. I look down at the lyrics in my lap. "I know where she was trying to get to. This song is about her. And this part, about going as far as she can go, that's about going to San Francisco. It's a joke we had when we were kids. That's where she wanted to go. That's where she would be if she hadn't . . ." I can't say it.

"I think it's time to let go," Sean says.

Sean's phone starts vibrating again. "Ah *there* it is." He snatches it off the seat and hits *Ignore*. He slips it in his pocket. And then he takes both of my hands in his and puts them over his heart. "That part of your life is over now," he says.

Back in the room, I drift in and out of a thick heavy sleep that paralyzes my limbs and fills my head with crazy dreams. Fast flashes of brilliant colors intersperse with slow-moving images, almost white, like a video made on a too-sunny day. Moments from real life, real memories, and made-up ones mix themselves together — Nina and I at a birthday party eating cake with our hands. Nina and I trying on dresses at Attic. Sean and Nina playing tag. Sean and I in bed in the hotel. Sean standing on a chair in this very hotel room, pushing something in between the blankets at the top of the closet, looking down to make sure I'm not awake to see him. Nina and I toasting each other in a fancy restaurant. Nina and I running away from home. Nina and I together in France. Nina in a car with Sean's brother, driving away from the house we grew up in, waving, waving, waving good-bye.

# THIRTY-SIX

I do not have the luxury of forgetting. There is no moment of blank calm, no moment of peace before reality catches up. I awake as the sun rises, and know exactly where I am and exactly what has happened. I'm crying before I open my eyes. This is the first morning I've had to know it. Yesterday seems hazy, like a dream, but this morning I have woken up with a clear mind at the bottom of a well. Now this is real. And I have to deal with it.

It is time to tell my mother.

I can hear the sound of rushing water coming from the bathroom.

I get out of bed. How will I even find my mother's number? It's in Sean's phone. I called her from his phone before. And I will do it again now. He won't mind. Of course he won't.

Sean is singing in the shower, loudly and terribly. His phone is on the desk.

I pick it up and go to the call log. There's my mother's number right there. I'm about to tap it, when I realize something strange. Something so strange my heart is pounding before I'm even done processing. I look at the call log more closely: There's the incoming call from Unavailable that I answered in the car last night. And before that there's a call to voice mail. And then there's my call to my mother on Tuesday morning. And before that, there's a number Sean called on Saturday a few hours after we started driving to Nebraska. The number looks weirdly familiar.

But there were no other calls made on this phone between my call to my mother and the call I made last night except for the one call to voice mail at 12:33 yesterday afternoon. Which is right around when Sean told me Nina was dead. One call to voice mail when Sean said he was calling the investigator.

So when did Sean talk to him exactly?

The phone starts buzzing in my hand. *Unavailable* is calling again.

"Hello?" I whisper.

For a moment, there is silence, and then a voice, whispering back. "Are you alone?"

The rushing water has stopped. Sean is out of the shower.

"Are you alone?" the voice says again.

"Yes," I whisper. My hands are sweating. "Who is this?"

"Is this Ellie?"

I freeze at the sound of my name. "Who is this?" I ask again.

"You called me the other day," the voice says. "You were looking for your sister. My name is Max and I know her . . ." The bathroom door opens a crack, a trail of steam escaping. It looks like smoke. ". . . and Sean did, too."

"Wh —" But before I can get any words out the bathroom door opens.

I hang up the phone and toss it quickly onto the bed just as Sean emerges from the bathroom, his hair damp, a towel wrapped around his waist, another hanging around his neck.

"You're up," he says.

"I'm up." I am sick with panic, but somehow manage to twist my mouth into something resembling a smile.

"Well, you seem like you're feeling a little better this morning."

"Yeah," I say. "Maybe a tiny bit."

The guy I called from Attic, the guy whose phone number Nina wrote on her drawing, has just called me on Sean's phone from a blocked number. Suddenly, something occurs to me. I grab my cutoffs off the floor, fish the cardboard credit card out of my back pocket. The number Nina wrote on the drawing is the same number Sean called on Saturday a few hours after we left my house.

*What the hell does all this mean?*

It means Sean has been hiding some things. And maybe lying about some things, too.

With that simple thought, I realize something else: The guy on the phone said he *knows* Nina. Not *knew* her. *Knows* her. Is it possible that . . . ?

The room tilts and spins.

Sean is right in front of me now, his chest dotted with beads of water.

"What are you looking at that for?" Sean is staring down at the drawing clutched in my hand.

"I don't know," I say.

"I don't think this is helping you, Ellie." Sean snatches the card from my hand. The sketch Nina drew of me is staring back at me. I look scared.

Sean walks toward the bathroom.

"Wait!" I say.

"This is for your own good," he calls out.

"WAIT!"

He closes the door behind him, a second later I hear the toilet flush.

Sean comes back into the bedroom. "After Jason died there were certain things I held on to, things that reminded me of him, and I couldn't move on until I let them go." He reaches out to stroke my face. "I think it will help you not to have that around," he says. Then he takes the towel from around his neck and starts rubbing his damp head. I stare at him. Who is this person I have spent the last five days with? Who I have shared a bed with? I suddenly feel like I've never seen him before in my life.

His left arm is up behind his head, the skin between his elbow and his armpit covered in those thin white scars. I remember tracing them with my fingers three nights ago when we got drunk in the hotel room. I remember thinking they were beautiful in their chaos. But as I stare at them now, they begin to look different. They are not chaos at all, there's an order to them, a pattern in the jumble.

Letters. These are letters. Carved in and then covered over with hatch marks, as though he was trying to hide them. But when you know what to look for, they come through. Four letters. Carved into his skin.

NINA.

*Max said he knew her, too.*

I can't breathe.

I want to be imagining this. But now that I've seen it, it's impossible to un-see it. Her name, there it is. It was there all along.

"I think I'm going to take a shower," I manage to say.

"Okay." Sean puts his arms around me. His skin is warm but touching him gives me chills. Over his shoulder, I see the blankets up at the top of the closet. I remember my dream last night, which maybe wasn't a dream at all . . .

"Could you go and get us some food?" I say. "I mean, while I'm in the shower."

Sean smiles. "You're hungry? That's a good sign."

"I'm starving."

"What do you want? Name anything and I'll go and get it."

"A salad," I say. "A really giant salad, with a lot of things in it."

"For breakfast?"

I nod.

"Okay, I'll have it for you when you get out." He sounds so pleased then, that I'm asking him for something, that it's something he's able to give me.

I nod, and force another smile. I manage to keep my knees from buckling until the bathroom door is closed safely behind me. I wait, my ear pressed against the door until I hear the outside door slam shut.

# THIRTY-SEVEN

There is no time to think.

I drag the heavy desk chair over to the closet, climb up, and stick my hands between the extra blankets on the top shelf. A few inches in, my hands hit leather. *So I wasn't dreaming after all.* I reach in farther, it's a handle. I grab it and pull out Sean's leather messenger bag. It feels warm, alive, like whatever's in here has a pulse of its own.

I jump off the chair and crouch down on the floor.

The bag is locked with a five-dial combination lock with letters on each of the dials. The lock is sturdy and the leather of the bag is thick.

My only hope is to unlock it with a guess. I rotate the tiny dials as fast as I can:

N-I-N-A-W

*No.*

J-A-S-O-N

*No.*

A-N-G-R-Y

*No.*

A-B-C-D-E

*No.*

S-E-A-N-L

*No.*

N-O-S-A-J

*No.*

W-A-N-I-N

*Now what?!*

I take a deep breath and a thought pops into my head. That bathroom wall back in Nebraska. Nina's graffiti. Cakey ❤'s J. CAKEY.

I turn the tiny dials one by one. I am all sweating palms and
pounding heart.

C-A-K-E-Y

I hold my breath and pull down on the lock.

It pops.

I open the bag and dump its contents onto the floor. There's
the newspaper article about Jason's death, a pile of envelopes, a
drawing, and a photograph. I pick up the photo. It's of Nina
and . . . I look closely. It's Sean's brother, Jason.

In the photo Nina and Jason are sitting behind a dining
room table with their arms around each other, smiles big and
brilliant. The remnants of a party are scattered in front of them:
wrapping paper, a big pile of what look like pink Hostess Sno
Balls, beer bottles, plastic cups. Also on the table is a snowboard
covered in ink drawings, with a bow on top. The wall behind
them is silver painted with a black rocket ship.

I've seen this wall before. This photo was taken at the
Mothership.

I flip the picture over. In Nina's handwriting: *I love you J.*

*J as in Jason.*

I move on to the drawing.

It's of Nina and a guy, hugging. And one of his arms is a duck. I smile, because this is so very Nina. But the strangest thing is that it's addressed to Sean . . . Nina drew this for Sean?

I look more closely.

No . . . no she did not.

This is of Nina and Jason. Sean took the drawing meant for Jason and he changed the name so he could pretend it had been drawn for him.

It's possible I'm going to throw up.

I let the paper fall from my hand and look down at the letters. There are dozens of them.

I pick up the one on top. My hands are shaking.

*Dearest Nina,*

*I understand how hard all of this must be for you, but I hope you know that I truly meant everything I said at Jason's funeral. I am here for you now, to lean on, to talk to, for whatever you need. I am here for you with all my heart, and I will always be here. No matter what. I don't actually know where I'm going to send this letter because I don't know where you are right now. But I'm sure you'll be back soon so I guess I'll just keep this for you. I want us to go through this together Nina. We need each other now more than ever.*

*With love,*

*Sean*

Jason, SEAN
even if you had ducks for
arms, I would still love you.
Sincerely, Cakey xx

Oh my God. I flip through the stack.

Nina,

I went to the Mothership again looking for you today. I don't understand why you'd leave and not tell me where you went? We need each other now. We are supposed to be going through this together!! No one else can understand you the way I can. No one else can be here for you now the way I can be. Why won't you let me?

Nina, I went to the Mothership last night. Some guy said he thought you'd been staying there but that you were gone now. He hadn't seen you in days. Where are you? Where are you? Where are you? I need to find you. Nothing makes any sense anymore. You need me now. YOU NEED ME! Why don't you understand that?

Nina, the police came to my house today to ask me questions about where Jason might have gotten the heroin. I told them that I had no idea. But where would they have gotten the idea that I would?

Nina,
I called your house today looking for you. Your mother got angry and told me to stop calling. It's been almost two entire weeks since Jason went away. I've been trying not to sleep, because when I do the screaming starts inside my head and it doesn't stop. I can't get you out of my head. I feel like maybe you have an idea what I did. But anything I did, I only did for us. You must know that. Come back to me.

I flip a few letters ahead.

It's been a month now. Where are you? Every night, when I lie down, he's back and he's begging me not to do it. But time is all funny and really the decision has already been made. I try and explain to him that I had to for love! But he doesn't understand and in the dream I

211

don't understand, either. When I wake up, it makes less sense than it used to. Where are you? Where are you, sweet Nina? We are supposed to be going through this together. If we're not, <u>THEN WHAT WAS THE POINT?</u>

I feel sick now, most of the time. It has invaded all my thoughts and everything I do. I can't get away from it. You are the only person who could make me forget, who could make me remember why this is okay, why I had to do this.

I go places where I think you'll be and wait for you to come back. This is all I can do now. Wait. Wait to pass the time and write you these letters, which I'll show you when I finally find you. WHERE ARE YOU!?!?!?! I want to believe you are lost, and I can help you find your way home. I am trying to have faith, but it is hard to have faith when I'm alone. I am trying.

WHERE HAVE YOU GONE! I can't take it anymore. I can't take it. I can't be without you. WHERE ARE YOU? I am sick every night and every day. I know you love me! I know you love me! I know it I know it. But why can't I feel it anymore? Something is fading. When the love is gone other things rise to the surface. Things I can't think about. I will never be able to stop without you.

My hands are shaking so hard the pages are rustling. I breathe in sharp gasps. There are too many letters here, too many for me to read them all. I flip to the last page in the stack. Five words. Stark black. All alone:

I DID IT FOR YOU

I let out a cry and raise my hand to my lips. No no no no no no no no. This is not possible. This cannot be real.

I pick up the newspaper clipping about Jason's death and I check the date. I can't believe I missed this before: Jason died the day Nina disappeared.

I need this not to mean what it seems like it means.

I think back to the party at the Mothership. To everything Sean ever said to me there. He wore a mask to the party. So no one would recognize him.

I hear the sound of a car pulling up outside. I grab the letters in handfuls and stuff them all back into the bag and then lock the lock. I climb up, lift the bag overhead. I push it in between the blankets right where it was, lean back slightly, almost topple off the chair. I look at the door. The chain is broken. And there is no second lock.

*What do I do? What the hell do I do now?*

He doesn't know what I've seen. And I have to keep it that way.

*He thinks I was in the shower.*

I tear off my clothes and run into the bathroom. I turn on the water. It's ice cold. I climb into the tub, drench my hair, my face. When my whole body is wet, I jump out. I hit my ankle against the leg of the sink. Hard. My eyes tear up. I wrap a towel around myself. I turn the water off. Run back, dripping. I hear Sean calling to me through the door. "Baby, can you hear me? I think I forgot the key! Ellie?"

He can't get in!

I start to reach for the motel phone on the nightstand.

Just as I hear, "Found it!" and the sound of a key in the lock.

And the door swings open.

Sean smiles. "Didn't you hear me calling you?" he asks. "I couldn't find my key, but then I did." He holds it up and wiggles it between his fingers. "Are you okay? You look so scared." The water is dripping onto the floor, pooling around my feet. My ankle is throbbing. He comes toward me.

"Aw, sweetie," Sean says. He puts a plastic bag down on the desk. "I'm sorry I left you alone for so long. Don't worry, I won't do it again."

He presses his body against mine, holding me to him. "You're shaking," says Sean. He rubs my arms.

"I'm cold," I say.

"Do you want to get dressed?" His voice is soft and gentle, like he's talking to a child.

I will go into the bathroom and put on my clothes. And then what?

*And then what?*

"And then you can come and eat your salad," Sean says.

I gather my clothes, bring them into the bathroom. I watch myself in the mirror as I slip my shirt over my head, pull up my shorts. I look terrified.

I come back into the bedroom. Sean has put the salad out on the desk next to a napkin and a plastic fork. There is a bottle of apple juice, too. He's taken the cap off.

"For you, my love," he says. He pats the chair.

His phone starts vibrating. He reaches into his pocket and stops it. I stare at his hands. He pulls out the chair for me. I sit. I stare down into the plastic bowl at a pile of vegetables covered in a slick of sour-smelling vinegar. I stab the fork into a piece of tomato. A piece of corn is stuck to the side, like a small rotting tooth. I gag.

"You okay?" Sean says.

"Yeah," I say. I put the tomato in my mouth, chew the cold flesh. Flesh. I gag again. I taste bile. Sean is standing over me. He puts his hand on my shoulder.

"I understand," he says. "I couldn't eat for almost a month after my brother died, but it will really make you feel better."

My thoughts zip inside my brain. I think of all the things he did since I met him, all the things he said that make sense in a whole new way now. I think of him gazing into my eyes. Telling me how much I look like her.

"I know how hard it is, baby." Sean reaches out and strokes my hair. "I'm so glad I can be here for you now." He crouches down so his head is level with mine and he puts his hands on my cheeks and turns me to face him. "You are in my heart now, Ellie." He looks me in the eyes. "And that's forever." He starts to lean in for a kiss. And then, without meaning to, I flinch, ever so slightly.

He pulls away. "Oh God," he says. "That look you just gave me." He stands and stumbles backward. "You know."

"What look?" I'm shaking my head. "What are you talking about?"

"You *know*," he says.

His face is changing now, in slow motion, his mouth opening, closing, and opening, his eyes clouding. It's too late. It's too late.

"No, no, no, no, no, no, no," he says. "Oh God, I'm so stupid. I should have known . . . you went into the bathroom to shower with all your clothes on, but when I came back, your clothes were all around the room. And . . ."

He walks slowly over to the closet, reaches up into the blankets and takes the bag down. He stares at the lock, his back to me. ". . . And these are not the letters I left the lock on." He looks up at me. "Do you know how I know?" He waits for me to answer. I am silent. "Because I left the lock turned to E-L-L-I-E. *I trusted you to trust me and you didn't!*"

I should get up. I should run. But I am frozen in my seat.

I feel his hand on my shoulder. My stomach drops.

He turns me around in the chair, bends down, gathers me into his arms, squeezes me, tighter, tighter, and tighter. He pulls me off onto the floor so we're crouched facing each other. It hurts how hard he's holding me.

"Oh, Ellie," he says over my shoulder. He sounds like he's crying now. He is shaking. He strokes my hair. "Do you love me, Ellie?"

I swallow. "Of course I do." My heart is pounding so hard I can feel it in my toes, in my teeth.

He mashes our faces together in an approximation of a kiss. His tears run down my cheeks.

"No, you don't," he says.

"Of course I do," I say. But it sounds like a lie, even to me.

"It's so unfair. So incredibly, terribly, horribly unfair. One mistake! I made one mistake in my entire life, and it ruins everything! I guess that's the funny thing about a mistake like that, you can't take it back. And here's the worst part, it wasn't even my mistake! Nina made me do it for her. I didn't want to do it. She set it up so that I'd think I had to! I loved her and she knew it, and I know she loved me. Or at least she could have if she let herself. But then he wasn't around and she still wouldn't be with me!" His eyes are filling up again. "She tricked me!"

He clenches his jaw, a vein throbs near his temple.

"It's going to be okay," I say.

"No," Sean says. A tear escapes his left eye and slides down to his chin. "It's not." He grabs my wrists. "I don't want to do this." He lets out a choked cry. "Please know that I really, really don't want to!"

He pushes me forward and wrenches both my arms behind my back. Then drags me back onto the chair. I try to pull away. I can't.

"What are you doing?" I say.

I feel something being wrapped around my wrists and tied tight to the back of the chair. His belt I think. "Don't go anywhere," Sean says, as though I actually could. And then he is out the door, running through the parking lot. I struggle against the belt. "Help!" I shout. "HELP!" But no one comes.

Sean's phone starts vibrating again on the desk. I lean over and with my chin, I knock the phone to the floor where it lands face down. I stretch out my leg as far as it will go, pull the phone toward me with my foot, and flip it over with my toe. It's still vibrating. I hit the *talk* icon. "HELP!" I shout toward the phone. I look down, pray it's Unavailable calling again, but there on the screen is a random number I don't recognize.

"Hello?" There's a faint voice coming through the phone. "Hello?" The voice calls again. My heart explodes in my chest. Is this . . . Could it really be . . .?

Sean is back. I kick his phone as he enters the room, and it slides under the desk behind the trash can.

"Do you want to know something, Ellie? Something I've never told anyone before?" The tears are falling faster now, an unreal amount of them. He has one arm behind him. "He didn't just go to sleep." Sean shakes his head and wipes his nose with the back of his hand. "That's how I thought it would be for him, y'know? Like going to sleep. But it wasn't. I went into his room and I held him down. He was a really heavy sleeper and didn't even wake up when the needle went in. But at the last second, he opened his eyes and looked at me. He had this look of *horror* on his face, Ellie. His last moment on this earth was spent *knowing* what I did to him." Sean inhales deeply and takes his arm from behind his back. There's something in his hand. Stark black barrel, shining dully under the motel's fluorescent lights. A gun, like something out of a movie. Sean looks down at it, then back up at me, then down at the gun again. "I got this for myself," Sean says. "For, y'know." He raises the gun to his head, jerks his head to the side, and then sticks out his tongue.

He smirks, amused at himself. "At first I couldn't take it, the guilt. And Nina was gone and I was trying to handle it alone. Then, Thanksgiving break, a few months after it happened, I came home from boarding school. Normally we would spend Thanksgiving at our house in Big Sur, which, hey, you'll think this is funny, that's actually the house where that band dropped your sister, but anyway, we didn't go that year because it was like my brother's favorite place on earth and my dad and stepmom thought it would be too hard to be there without him. So it was just the three of us at my house sitting at that giant table, staring at our plates, at all this food the cook made that we weren't eating. And I . . . I *missed* him, which was so crazy. I started thinking about how different dinner would have been if he was there. And how cool he was and how funny he was. It was like that was the first time he really felt like a brother to me and it made me sick, so I excused myself, which no one really minded. And I went up to my room and I got the gun out of this box in my closet. I wasn't even sure I knew how to load it right. I watched this tutorial thing online but it's not like I really had any chances to test out shooting before. So I did what the video said and then I held the gun up to my face and I was about to squeeze the trigger when suddenly it was like someone was talking to me directly inside my head. I don't know if it was God or my brother's ghost, but the voice told me not to do it, not to kill myself, because that wouldn't make things right. I wasn't really the one at fault there, see. I wasn't even the one that killed him, they were my hands, but doing what *she* wanted. Your sister was the one who did it to him." Sean presses his lips together. "It was her fault and I was the only person on earth who knew that. Before that I'd been looking for your sister for months. But after that I stopped looking and I just waited. I knew if I waited long enough, I'd get a chance to make things right because it was fate that I should. It was hell, all that waiting. But I never lost faith and I never gave up hope and then when I finally saw you at that party that night at the Mothership, I knew my wait was over and that you'd been sent there for me, to lead me to her, to help me fix everything. But then I started falling in love with you." Sean tips his head to the side and smiles. "And I thought that maybe *that* was the reason I was at that party, not to find Nina after all, but to find you. So I thought if we could let the past go, then it would all be okay. That's why I told you she died, so we could move on . . . together."

Sean stares me straight in the eye. And leans in closer. "Do you know what I've been through, Ellie? Can you even imagine? You think you have suffered for love? *I have suffered for love* and so there I was, waiting for the love I've earned to come back to me. And then there you were. Dear, sweet, beautiful you who looks so much like her, only you look at me differently than she ever did, and then when you told your friend to leave I knew you loved me in a way she never had. You are the reason I knew it was okay to let her go. Because I had you now. Someone to look at me the way you did. But *you are not looking at me like that anymore.*" Sean's nose is practically touching mine now. His jaw muscles twitch.

"I'm sorry," I say quietly.

"Look at me like that again, please, Ellie," He is begging. "Please just look at me like that again, the way you did before."

And I try. I try to look at his face and see what I saw before I knew the truth.

"I disgust you," Sean says. His breath is hot on my face. "I didn't have a choice, Ellie." He takes a quivering breath. "Tell me you understand why I had to do what I had to do!"

"I understand why you had to do what you had to do," I say.

"And tell me you understand why I have to do what I have to do next," he says. There are tears in his eyes,

My whole body goes cold. "What do you have to do next?"

"You already know," Sean says. "I already told you the story."

"The story?"

"The one about Nina in the parking lot."

"But that didn't actually happen!"

"That didn't actually happen . . ." A tear drips down each cheek. "Yet."

My mouth drops open. I cannot speak.

"I don't want to do it," Sean says. He stomps his foot. "I mean, you know that, right? I'll do you here first so you don't have to watch, and then head off to San Francisco on my own after you're . . ."

"Are you talking about . . ." My voice is a whisper now. ". . . killing me?"

Sean looks down at the floor. "Well, when you put it that way, it sounds so harsh." Sean smiles this funny little smile. And then he bursts into tears. He sobs in ragged gasps, his shoulders shaking, then picks his head back up and wipes his eyes with the heel of his hand. "This is what I have to do now. I wish I had a choice . . ."

"But you do!" I say.

"No," Sean says. "I could never let you go. You'd tell people and then I'd never be able to make things right." Sean is pointing the gun straight at me. He stands up and steps back. "And even if you didn't, you don't love me anymore and you think I'm some monster. And I couldn't live knowing that you think such terrible things about me. I couldn't stand it." His hands are shaking. I strain against the belt again, but it's too tight. I can't move. I stare at the gun. I cannot believe this is real. I cannot believe this is real.

I cannot believe it ends like this.

"I have to get this over with." His voice is calmer now. He's talking to himself. "I have to do it and get it over with." He wraps his arms around my shoulders, and squeezes me. "Just please," he whispers. "Keep your eyes closed, okay?"

I have ten seconds left on this earth. He lets go, kisses me on the top of the head, squeezes me again, hard. Five seconds.

"Sean, wait!"

Four seconds.

"I can't."

Three seconds.

"WAIT!"

Two seconds.

"I'm really sorry, sweetie."

Sean takes a deep breath. He cocks the trigger.

One second.

"Close your eyes," he says.

# THIRTY-EIGHT

"Sean, I LOVE YOU!"

Sean freezes, his arm stuck straight out in front of him.

*"What?"*

My whole body is shaking. "Sean, don't kill me," I shout. "I love you! Do whatever you want to Nina. I don't care! I only care about you."

Something flickers across his face.

"You're just saying that," he says, "to get me to let you go." But he wants to believe me, I can tell he wants to believe me.

"No," I say. "I don't *want* you to let me go! *I want to be with you.*"

"Then why . . . then why were you acting like that? Why were you looking at me like that before?"

"I was jealous! When I saw those letters, it made me feel sick! Because I was jealous and I wanted you to be able to love *me* that much."

Sean frowns. "But why did you go into my bag then?"

"Because I love you!" I say. "And I was feeling insecure." I pause. "And I was worried that maybe that person who calls you all the time and hangs up really *is* another girl and the idea of it makes me want to vomit and I want you all to myself! I wanted to make sure there was no one else!"

And Sean has no idea what to think now. I can see it on his face.

I go on. "I don't care about Nina or your brother or anyone! I understand why you did what you did! It was only because you're so passionate, because you really know how to love people. Because you really love with all your heart! So I don't care what you do to Nina because I love you and that means you're my family now. And I am your family. And we don't need anyone else."

Sean leans forward.

"You really love me?" He sounds so desperate.

"More than anyone I've ever known."

He lowers the gun and leans in even closer. Our foreheads are touching.

"I'll still need to go to San Francisco and take care of Nina, you understand that, right? I don't think I'll be able to move on until I do. It's not fair for her to be alive when he isn't. And I won't be free until everything is even. Until I make it even." He sounds so calm now.

"Of course," I say. "She deserves it. Whatever happens to her, she brought it on herself."

He leans back. "So you'll come with me? You'll help me find her?"

I nod. "I'll go anywhere you want," I say.

"You think she'll still be there?"

"Oh yes," I say, and then loudly, "She's definitely still in San Francisco. And I know where to start looking for her when we get there, too. Right on Haight Street. We'll find a clue as to where she is, right on Haight Street. So we'll be there in about twelve hours, I guess. Or maybe thirteen. And we'll go right there to Haight Street."

He's not crying anymore, his eyes look huge, oddly beautiful, in that way sick things can.

This is my last and only hope. I slow my breathing. Inside I am screaming, but my face is calm. I stare into his eyes, trying to radiate love.

Time creeps by. One minute. Two minutes.

Finally, Sean lets out a huge sigh and his mouth curls into a strangely sweet smile. For a moment he looks about ten years old. "I love you more than I ever loved her," Sean says. "You don't have anything to worry about. That was just a fantasy, but this . . ." He presses his lips against mine. I feel the bile rise in my throat. He strokes the side of my face with the gun. ". . . This is real."

# THIRTY-NINE

I shift in my seat and gaze out at the soft blue arc of the sky stretching in every direction. We're two hours closer to San Francisco, speeding down a mostly empty highway.

Sean reaches down and takes his iced coffee out of the cupholder. His third of the trip so far. "I was supposed to go to San Francisco once, a long time ago," he says. His voice is gentle, like he's telling me a bedtime story. "My mom was going to take me, but we never quite made it there." He holds the straw up to my mouth, offering me a sip because my hands are tied behind my back. I shake my head. "It's kind of a funny story actually. So we were staying at my family's house in Big Sur. This was when it was just me and my dad and my actual mom. My mom didn't like to ski but my dad was out skiing every day, and I guess my mom was getting bored and lonely or maybe she was just mad at my dad, I don't know. But one night at like three in the morning she woke me up and told me we were going on vacation, her and me. She told me to get in the car because she'd already packed and everything and we needed to leave before traffic got bad. I was five at the time so I didn't think much of it, other than that it sounded fun, so I got into the car in my pajamas with my pillow and my blanket. After she started driving, she told me she had friends in San Francisco and that we should go and visit them because she hadn't seen them in twenty-five years and she wanted to show them how cute I was. After a while we stopped at an all-night mini-mart for ice cream and then kept driving. And I remember that she let me get *three* ice-creams bars which was basically the most exciting thing in the world. I don't remember much else after that except at some point later we were surrounded by about fifteen cop cars with their sirens and lights on. Turns out my mom had never mentioned her plan to my dad, so when he woke up the next morning and found the house empty, he freaked. And apparently she had been taking pills at the time, like tons and tons of prescription uppers that who even knows where she got them, and then I guess after that some amphetamines or whatever prescribed by Doctor Drug-dealer . . . so she ended up back in the rehab hospital place for a while after that, and then about nine months after *that* she went away for good. The best part of the story, though, is that later the maid was unpacking the bags my mom had put in the trunk and you'll never guess what was in them." He pauses. "Try and guess."

"Clothes?" I say.

"For me, she'd packed nothing but this tiny winter jacket that I'd worn when I was about two, a bunch of action figures, and a bunch of mini juice boxes. And for herself all she brought was," Sean starts laughing then. "A bag of . . . floor-length . . .

black-tie . . . ball gowns!" Tears are filling his eyes, he's laughing so hard. "These custom-made designer dresses, probably worth like a hundred thousand dollars." He hiccups, and wipes the tears off his cheeks. "According to my dad's version of the story, when the police finally found us, I was curled up in the backseat of the car, covered in ice cream, like basically catatonic I was so scared. But that's not how I remember it. I think it's probably my very favorite memory of my mom, actually." He pauses and takes a breath. "I guess you and I didn't pack that well, either, come to think of it. But anything we need we can get while we're there, since I figure we'll want to go . . . Hey, you know what we should do? We should go on a big shopping trip after . . ." Sean stops then, reaches down for his coffee again. He turns toward me and smiles this sweet sheepish smile, like he's just slightly embarrassed by what we're on the way to do.

The sun is high in the sky and the road is filled with other cars. Sean has one hand heavy on my knee. We are silent now.

They say that no matter what life throws at you, there's always something to be learned, and I sure have learned a lot in these last eight hours since we've been on the road, such as exactly what it feels like to spend the better part of a day sitting in a Volvo with your wrists tied together, and that I am, as it turns out, an incredible actress. Too bad my best and only performance is taking place in a car with an audience of one.

\* \* \*

The sun is setting now. Sean pulls over on a long stretch of highway surrounded on either side by giant fields of waist-high grass that no one has touched for years. "I'll be right back," he says. He gets out of the car, walks fifty feet into the middle of the field, and holds the gun straight up over his head. There's a loud *CRACK*. A delicate whisper of smoke curls from the barrel of the gun up toward the sky. Sean comes back to the car, gets in, and shuts the door.

"I just wanted to check," he says, "that it would work."

Sean starts the car again. We will be there soon.

I'm staring out the window at the early evening sky, at the swooping red cables of the Golden Gate Bridge lit by a thousand tiny lights and the sparkling ocean beyond it.

"It's beautiful," I say.

"It is," Sean says, the tension is back in his voice. Maybe it's the nine extra-large iced coffees. Maybe it's that what he's about to do is finally sinking in. "Haight Street?" Sean says. "That's where you said you think we'll . . ." Sean stops, for the last twelve hours he hasn't, not once, actually directly referred to what we've come here to do. "That's where you think we should go?" He turns toward me.

My organs, my bones, everything inside me, has dissolved into a pool of hot panic. But I nod calmly. "Oh yes," I say. "Haight Street, I'm sure of it."

Sean reaches into his pocket, then behind him into his seat, then leans down and sticks his hand between the seat and the door.

"Everything okay?"

"Yeah," Sean says slowly. "I can't find my phone."

"How weird," I say. "I hope you didn't leave it back at the motel."

"Me, too," Sean says.

I close my eyes and picture that phone, exactly where I kicked it. And I have to turn my face toward the window because at this moment it is impossible for me not to smile.

# FORTY

To everyone else out here we're just another young couple enjoying an evening stroll on Haight Street. No one can see the loaded gun shoved down the front of Sean's jeans. Or the red marks on my wrists where they were tied. Or the fact that Sean is crushing my fingers with his own, as though to keep me from running, as though he never plans on letting go.

A girl in a tiny yellow dress walks past us and smiles at Sean. When she gets a few feet away she turns around and looks back. Is it . . . ? No. She's just some girl who thinks he's cute. She sees what most people see when they look at him, a seventeen-year-old kid, with floppy hair and a heartbreakingly beautiful face. I used to see him like that, too.

"Whatcha looking at?" Sean asks.

"I'm glad we're here is all," I say.

He tries to smile. He's nervous. "Me, too," he says.

We keep making our way up the steep hill — we pass a fancy home goods store, a store that sells handblown glass pipes, a tapas restaurant, a place with psychedelic posters stuck up in the window.

We keep going. Sean squeezes my hand again. I can feel his heart beating through his fingers. Or maybe that's my own.

Everything we pass seems somehow meaningful. A man in a pair of very yellow pants walks by, struggling with grocery bags filled with fruit. A girl in a maroon hooded sweatshirt is very deliberately searching for something in her pocket. A man drops a bottle of water and it splashes out onto the street. He looks up, we make eye contact. He looks away. Two men in tuxedos are walking arm in arm.

"Hey, dude, can you spare a smoke?" There's a girl and a guy sitting cross-legged on the sidewalk. The girl has short black hair and purple eyeliner. "Or some change?"

"Sorry," I say. I look at her again . . . is she? She's not looking at us anymore. Sean and I keep going.

Finally we reach the top of the hill, and the street ends at the entrance to Golden Gate Park. There's a grassy area in the front, and behind it a paved pathway winding back. A young couple is leaning against a brick wall kissing. Three guys are tossing around a Frisbee. A girl is sitting playing acoustic guitar. Sean gasps suddenly, he grabs my upper arm, squeezes it.

"Ellie," he whispers. "Ellie." His hands are shaking. He motions toward a small group standing a few feet away. They're all a few years older than us. And all of them are wearing identical T-shirts, white V-necks with a graphic drawn in the center: a sweep of a jawline, the arch of an eyebrow, the crescent of a crooked smile.

It's a face: mine.

232

Sean leans in close. "Bingo," he whispers.

They look like they're waiting for someone. One of them — a girl with long dark hair — watches us approach.

"Hey," Sean says. "I really like your shirt."

"Yeah?" She has giant eyes rimmed in gold. "Thanks." She holds my gaze a little too long. "This local artist makes them."

A big guy steps forward. He's about six-five, with giant arm muscles bulging under the thin white fabric of his T-shirt. "We each got one."

"Awesome," Sean says, nodding. "Really cool." He pauses. "You don't happen to know where I might find the person who made the shirts, do you? We're from out of town and these would be great to bring back home. Like as souvenirs."

"I do indeed," the guy says. He turns around. He points to his back over his shoulder.

*NINA WRIGLEY DESIGNS:*

*Custom-Made Hand-drawn T-shirts.*

*1414 Avery Square, San Francisco, CA*

"She sells them out of her apartment," the guy says. "You can go right now, I bet she'll be there."

"Thanks, man," Sean says. He squeezes my hand. "Can you tell me how to get there? I lost my phone."

The guy glances at me, and then back to Sean. "I'll do you one better, I'll take you there myself."

Sean shakes his head. "Nah, that's okay, man. You don't need to do that."

"Oh, I don't mind," the guy says. "Let me!"

"No, seriously, you can't. I mean . . . we're not going to go tonight. We'll probably go tomorrow or the next day or something."

"Okay," the guy says, slowly. "Okay. Okay." He reaches into his pocket and takes out a little notepad and a pen. He scribbles down the directions. Sean is watching the guy. The girl behind him is still watching me. When our eyes meet again, something flickers across her face. The guy hands the directions to Sean.

We turn, and start walking. Sean is holding on to my arm, his entire body shaking. "Let's get this over with," he says. "We'll just go now, no stopping, no thinking. We'll go and then we'll find somewhere to sleep and then when we wake up tomorrow morning, this will all be behind us."

"Yes," I say to Sean. I am beside him, breathing in and out and in and out, reminding myself to have faith in her. To keep walking. And when the time comes, to be ready. "By tomorrow morning, everything will be different."

# FORTY-ONE

We turn right and head up a steep hill on a narrow street, surrounded by tall skinny houses on either side.

Sean's hand is on his stomach, holding on to the gun through his shirt. "This has already happened," he whispers. "All of this has already happened."

We turn right, then left, then right again. I think I hear footsteps behind us, but I'm too scared to turn.

Sean whispers, "I can't wait until this is all over."

"Me, neither," I whisper back. We keep going. The sky is dark. Without our phones, there is nothing but the yellow glow from the cracked streetlights to guide us.

Finally we're in front of a narrow gray house, with a heavy brass *1414* hung upon the blue front door. Sean grabs the doorknob. "This is it." He turns it. The door is unlocked. "Fate," Sean says.

He opens the door. There's a skinny staircase leading up with a white paper lantern dangling above. Sean takes the gun out from under his shirt with shaking hands. He whispers, "Go." And I start making my way up.

Right foot.

Left foot.

Right foot.

Left foot.

"Call her name now," he whispers.

I take a deep breath. "Nina," I call out.

"Louder," he says.

Right foot.

Left foot.

Right foot.

"NINA," I say again.

"Louder!"

Left foot.

Right foot.

"NINAAAAAA!" No answer. "NIIIIIINNNNNNNN-AAAAAA!!!!!"

Left foot.

Right foot.

Left foot.

"*Belly?*" We hear a voice coming through the door at the top of the stairs, very quiet, barely more than a whisper.

My heart stops.

"Belly? Is that you?"

Sean's breath catches in his throat.

I squeeze my eyes shut and breathe in deep. I smell orange and ginger. Nina.

I'm not scared anymore.

We reach the top of the stairs and push through the door. We're in a large living room — dark wood floors, big fluffy couches, framed drawings covering every last bit of wall space, and there, standing by herself in the center of the room, is my sister.

*My sister.*

Looking both exactly like and completely different from the person I remember.

Our eyes meet, and a warmth spreads outward from the center of my chest. When she sees me she starts to smile, but then she looks behind me, at Sean, and stops. Her jaw drops, her lips pull back. It's like she's screaming only no sound is coming out. I have never in my life seen Nina afraid before. But now, she is terrified.

*She is not supposed to be terrified.*

*She is not supposed to be fucking terrified!*

That final call that came in on Sean's phone back at the motel, the one that I answered with my feet, *I thought that was Nina.* I thought that was her voice calling out through the phone. And I thought she had heard everything Sean and I said after I kicked the phone under the desk. I thought she knew we were coming to Haight Street. And I thought she was leading us to her. I thought she was going to save us.

*But I was wrong.*

*Everything I thought was wrong.*

Sean is staring at her, his nostrils flared, his eyes glowing. He barely even looks human.

Her face is frozen.

He reaches for the gun inside his shirt. Everything is happening so fast.

"This is for what you did to me . . ." He sounds like he's reciting lines from a script he rehearsed in his head a thousand times. "This is for what you made me do to him."

He raises the gun between his shaking hands.

Nina just stands there.

The gun is pointing straight at her.

This is it.

*This is it.*

And then, there's an explosion. Not from the gun, but from within me.

*Nina is not the only one who can save us.*

Suddenly I am flying through the air, screaming, "LEAVE MY SISTER ALONE!" I stretch out my arm, catching Sean right under his chin. His head snaps back, hard. Then I slam my shoulders into the middle of his stomach with everything I've fucking got. We tumble to the floor. Sean lands on his back, a wheezy whistle escaping from his lips. The gun is knocked from his hand and slides spinning across the wood floor.

And for a moment we are all silent and completely still. I don't think a single one of us can quite believe what I've just done.

"FREEZE! PUT YOUR HANDS ABOVE YOUR HEAD!" Five uniformed police officers have materialized out of the shadows. They stand over us, their guns cocked and aimed at our heads. Sean turns to the side, the expression on his face one of such complete and utter bewilderment that for a second I almost feel sorry for him.

But just for a second.

"What's going on!?" he says. "Ellie? Ellie?!"

All I can do is shake my head.

A police officer yanks his arms behind his back and cuffs him. Another one starts to read him his rights. Two others lift him up, his body limp like a doll's, his head hanging down. His feet barely brush against the ground as he is carried backward toward the door.

But right before he is pulled through, he looks up, and there is a hint of something else on his face. Something that looks an awful lot like relief.

And then he is gone.

I look up. The wall behind Nina is covered in drawings, photo-realistic scenes from our lives growing up — the park where we used to play, our aunt's house at the beach, even a little picture of the guy from the Covered Wagon Shipping commercial. And in the center is a framed portrait of our mother. In the picture she looks different than I've seen her in a long time, soft and pleased and proud, as though this is how Nina's been remembering her.

I turn back toward Nina, who is standing right there in front of me. It took two years and two thousand miles, but I am finally here with her. Her bottom lip is shaking. Mine is shaking, too.

We open our arms then, Nina and I, and we crash together into a hug, a hug that feels like any of the thousands and thousands of other hugs we've shared in the last sixteen years, but also completely different because of all that it took to get here, because we almost didn't get to have this one. Neither of us says anything because words do not exist for a moment like this one. We just stand there hugging until the tears are pouring down both our faces.

# FORTY-TWO

What happens next is a blur, but there are certain details I know I will never forget — the sour human smell in the back of the police car, the sound of my mother's voice on the phone when they call her from the station, the buzz of the bright fluorescent lights in the room where I tell Detective Bryant a four-hour-long story about every single thing that happened in the five days since I first met Sean. But more than anything I know I will never forget the look on Nina's face when Detective Bryant comes into the waiting room where Nina and I sit on scratched-up wooden chairs to tell us that Sean confessed to everything. "We barely even questioned him," Detective Bryant says. He shakes his head. "That happens sometimes." And Nina just turns toward me, lips pressed together, eyes watering, her entire face contorted with such pure relief, I know I cannot even begin to understand the hell that preceded it.

"It's finally over," Nina whispers. And she squeezes my hand.

"You can both go home now," Detective Bryant says.

So we stand up and we walk outside. The clear early-morning sunlight shines on our faces. I can already tell it's going to be a beautiful day.

# FORTY-THREE

Everything out the window shrinks as we rise higher, houses, cars, mountains. My ears pop. I press my face against the glass.

"Wait, wait, wait, Belly," Nina says. "Don't move for one more second . . ." She holds her pen up to her lips and then brings the point back to the napkin she's been sketching on. "Your face is more angley than it was the last time I drew you." She holds the pen to her lips again. "More cheekboney."

"Maybe," I say. I glance at the napkin onto which she's sketching the outline of my face.

"No, definitely," she says. "You look older."

"Well . . . time will do that to a person, I guess," and I try to make my tone light and jokey but it doesn't come out that way. The problem is this: I know now that Nina is safe and I can see her. Nothing else matters; nothing else should matter. But after two years of wondering, my brain doesn't quite know how to stop.

"I can't believe Mom's taking the day off just to come meet us," Nina says. She shakes her head slowly. "I mean, when's that ever happened before, right?"

The unasked questions sit heavy in my mouth, and everything

else I try and say has to work its way around them. But after what my sister's been through, it doesn't feel fair. It doesn't feel fair to make her explain anything.

"Oh, Bel." Nina puts down her pen. "Please, just ask me, already, okay? I get that you need to ask me and it's fine, it really is. Just . . . ask me."

"How did you . . ."

"We're sisters," she says simply.

I take a deep breath. "I just want to understand why. And I know it's selfish to ask because of everything that you went through."

Nina lets out this wry little laugh and then shakes her head. "I'm not the only one who's been through something here, Bell. Need I remind you?"

I shake my head.

"You need to know, so I need to tell you." Nina takes a deep breath. "So here it goes. Three years ago I heard about a party at this crazy house called the Mothership. It was the middle of summer, but the party was supposed to be a Winter Wonderland thing because someone had gotten ahold of an industrial snowmaking machine and they put it in the backyard and turned that sucker on and left it running for two days straight. When I got to the party, everyone was outside going nuts: some girls were building an igloo and there were snowball fights everywhere, and some guy was making this ridiculous snowperson under a beach umbrella. So I had had this idea to make this sort of fuzzy pink dress for myself and dye my hair light pink, and be a Hostess Sno Ball, you know like the cake? So I did, and that's what I wore to the party, but everyone kept asking if I was cotton candy or a pink pom-pom or something.

"And then this guy came up to me, really cute, carrying this snowboard. And I'd noticed him before doing these insane snowboard tricks on this ramp they'd set up. Anyway, he turned to me and, I'll never forget this because it was the very first thing he ever said to me, he said, 'Someday I'll be telling our grandchildren how when I met their grandma she was dressed up like a snack cake.' And I know that could sound like a cheesy line or something but because of the way he said it and because it was about snack cakes, it didn't feel cheesy, it was just funny. And then I looked at him and I was like, 'Well, you know, by the time we have grandkids it'll be way in the future and snack cakes might not even exist anymore,' and he was like, 'Well, if that's true we should probably start stockpiling now, don't you think?' And that was the first conversation we ever had." Nina turns toward me, her eyes sparkling. "That was kinda it for me. We were together after that. We didn't have to talk about it or wonder about it, we just . . . were. So, one day Jason is telling me about his stepbrother and how he's kind of messed up and how he got sent away to boarding school and how really deep down he's a good kid." Nina shakes her head. "Jason saw the best in people." She looks back down at her napkin. "Jason said his stepbrother was going to be in town on break from school and he wanted me to meet him. And I was excited, actually. I mean, I had no idea where all this would . . ." Nina swallows hard. "I had no idea where all this would end up. But anyway, so I met Sean. I remember thinking right when I first met him that there was something really, I don't know, different about him, I guess. But I kind of liked that about him. You know what I mean?"

I nod. "I know exactly what you mean." And I smile wryly, because it's all so ridiculous.

Nina smiles wryly back. "He was really charming sometimes. Charming and weird and I thought, well, good for him for doing his own thing. And to be honest, at first I really liked having him around, it was nice having someone to be a big sister to." Nina tips her head to the side. "I missed *you* then, Belly. But you were always so mad at me around that time."

"I'm sorry." I say. "I wished you were around more then, I guess, and I didn't really know how to express it."

"I know that now," Nina says. "What I'm trying to say is that I was thinking of him like a little brother. But he didn't see it that way. He got this crush on me. Right at the beginning I thought it was just kind of innocent and sweet." Nina takes a breath, "It didn't take too long to realize it wasn't.

"He started writing me these letters from school, like really, really, really long letters, full of all this stuff about how one day we'd be together, and how we were soul mates and how much he loved me. And no matter what I said or did, he couldn't be convinced otherwise. It's like the more I told him we were never going to be together, the harder he tried to impress me. He bought some heroin this one time. I don't even know where he got it, but he had it with him when he came home for winter break. I remember when he showed it to me, he was so excited about it, like I was going to be so impressed." Nina shakes her head. "Needless to say, I wasn't."

"Fast-forward to the next summer, two summers ago, right after Jason and I both graduated. It was Jason's eighteenth birthday, and his best friend, Max, was in town staying at the Mothership, which is where he always stayed when he was visiting, and so we were having a little birthday party there for Jason. It was just me and Jason and Max and a few other people hanging out. And I had gotten this snowboard for Jason that I knew he would love. It was expensive though, I had to get a credit card so I could pay for it. And I knew he'd never let me get him such a fancy present," Nina smiles, "so I drew all over it so there was no way he could return it. And I'll never forget his face when he opened it, he couldn't stop smiling." Nina smiles at the memory. "He said it was the very best present he'd ever gotten and asked if I would take a trip cross-country with him for our one-year anniversary, which was in about a month, at the end of July. He said we'd pack up his old blue Volvo and hit the road, crashing with friends on the way, and then we could stay at his stepdad's house in Big Sur and he'd teach me to snowboard and we could give his present its first trip down the mountain together."

"Wait, Jason had a blue Volvo?" I tip my head to the side.

"Yup," Nina says. And then she tips her head to the side, too. "Was that what Sean was driving when . . ." I nod.

"Go on," I say.

"It was around three-thirty in the morning and Jason and

247

I were getting ready to leave the Mothership so he could drive me home, but we were both being really slow about it, I think because neither one of us wanted the night to end. I mean, it really had been the most wonderful, perfect, amazing night. And that's when Sean showed up, acting all casual like it was the most normal thing in the world for him to be there. The Mothership was about twenty miles from their house and Sean had walked there. To see me. Jason wasn't mad or anything, because he never really got mad, he was just worried about Sean and didn't want him to get in trouble for sneaking out and wanted to get him back home as soon as possible. At that point I felt like it would probably be better if I wasn't even in the car with them, so I said I'd just stay over at the Mothership. I always tried to make sure I was back home by the time the sun came up, but that night it seemed like the only other choice was a really bad one. So Jason came over and said good-bye and that he'd come back and pick me up in the morning and he'd get the snowboard then, too. And then he gave me a quick hug and we didn't even kiss or anything because Sean was standing there glaring at us. They walked out waving. And then at the last second Jason stuck his head back in the door and said something about how we could get waffles in the morning, and then he mouthed 'I love you' . . ." Nina looks down. ". . . And that was it."

"So that was the last time you . . ."

Nina nods. And takes a deep breath. She wipes her face quickly with her hands, because she's crying a little, and I wipe my face with my hands because as it turns out, I am crying a little, too. "The next morning I called Jason and he kept not picking up his phone and I was figuring he left his phone on silent or something. So I kept calling and calling. And then finally his mom answered."

Nina looks up at me. "She sounded really weird on the phone, it was like I was talking to this robot or something who'd been programmed to sound like her. I was trying hard to be extra friendly because I always had the feeling she didn't like me. I was saying something about the wallet she'd gotten for Jason for his birthday, how nice it was and everything but she cut me off. And she asked me if I'd seen Jason the day before and I said yeah, that I had. And that we'd had a birthday party for him. And then she said, and I remember, these are her exact words, she said, 'Well, Nina, your little birthday party killed him.' And at first I somehow didn't even think she meant literally, I thought she must have meant she thought he was really hungover or something, which didn't even make any sense because he knew he was going to have to drive, so he hadn't been drinking. But then she started saying all this stuff about the preliminary autopsy reports and how they suggested a heroin overdose. And it was obvious from the way she said it that she thought it was my fault."

"But how could she even think that at all!" I say.

"Her son had just died, Belly," Nina says. "I'm not sure you can blame someone for anything they're thinking in a situation like that."

And I stop and I nod, because I realize that I've had the tiniest taste of what that might feel like when I thought Nina was dead, and I don't think I'd even begun to really feel it yet.

"So here was Jason's mom telling me he was gone, and I still somehow didn't even understand what she was saying. I kept

249

thinking that they must have made a mistake and maybe he was only sleeping. And then finally she said that she had to go and she hung up. My head basically exploded then and I don't remember much of what happened for a while. I stayed at the Mothership basically catatonic until the funeral.

"It wasn't until after the funeral was over that I got to thinking about some things. Like how I knew Jason would never have done heroin in a trillion years, and how Sean had gotten some up at school that time. And then I started thinking about how Sean had acted at the wake. I had this vivid memory of him sitting next to me on the couch, rubbing my back, and telling me how he and I needed each other now that Jason was gone. And that Jason would have wanted us to go through this together. And even though I felt like something weird was definitely going on, I still couldn't even imagine that Sean would have done what he did.

"But then something else happened. There was this girl named Jeannie who I'd met at the Mothership. She was this funny girl from Texas with a thick Texas accent and was in town for a few days. But she was there the night of Jason's party, and after Jason died, she came to his funeral. So she was hanging out with me at the Mothership the day after and the two of us were sitting out front and she was comforting me and I guess she had her arm around me or something. And I remember looking up and there was Sean walking up the driveway, and he was glaring at her with this *hatred*. The next day she was driving back to Texas and she got in a car accident and the insurance company investigator said someone had messed with her brakes. Thank God she was wearing her seat belt so she was basically fine, but *that's* when it all finally clicked in my head. When I found out about Jeannie, I suddenly realized what had happened." Nina leans back in her seat.

"So what did you do?"

"Well, as soon as I realized what happened I went to the police. But all they said was that they'd 'look into it.'" Nina makes air quotes with her fingers. "It was obvious that they thought I was crazy and weren't taking me seriously and probably weren't going to do a damn thing. So I went to his mom and stepdad and tried to explain but they wouldn't talk to me. Meanwhile, I was still staying at the Mothership then. I didn't feel like I could leave or come home, I was too messed up. Sean kept coming by to see me and finally I hid in the basement so everyone would think I wasn't there anymore. But then I kept thinking about you and about Mom, and how if Sean was capable of killing his own brother to get to me, and would slice some girl's brakes just because she'd put her arm around me once, then what would he do to the other people I cared about the most? Wouldn't killing you guys make me *need* him? And isn't that what he wanted? So I decided the only thing I could do that would make everyone safe would be to leave . . ." Nina pauses. "So that's what I did."

She turns toward me, her eyes wet. "I am so, so, so sorry for what you must have gone through. But I know you, Belly, and I knew if you had any idea about what was going on, you'd have insisted on trying to help me."

"Of course I would have," I said.

"But I also knew if you tried to help me at all, you weren't safe. So I decided it was much better for you to miss me and still be around to miss me . . . So before Max left and went back home, he'd invited me to come stay with him in Denver for a while if I wanted to. And I didn't know what else to do with myself, so I got on a bus and I went. I'd written his phone number down on this little cardboard credit card thing that I'd been using as a bookmark but then I ended up forgetting it back at the Mothership. So when I got to Denver I didn't even know where to go at first and I had no money and I lost my credit card on the bus and had to cancel it. I ended up at this tattoo place because its name reminded me of you, actually, and then I got this, in honor of Jason." Nina leans forward and pulls the neck of her tank top down slightly, revealing three tiny numbers inked in black right over her heart. "Jason's birthday," Nina says, tapping it. "The way he was on this day, *this* is how I want to remember him." Nina lets go of her shirt and takes a deep breath. "And then I ended up staying with the woman who owned the tattoo shop for like a week before I was able to get in touch with Max. After that I worked for her for a while. But it's like here I was in Denver, pretending my head was screwed on to my body when it was floating a hundred miles up in the sky. I'd wake up every morning and forget where I was and who I was and that Jason wasn't with me anymore. I felt like I needed to *do* something, you know, like to really say good-bye. And I had the snowboard I'd given him with me, because I didn't know what else to do with it. So I thought about how excited Jason had been to bring the snowboard to Big Sur and give it a trip down the mountain and how he'd always wanted to teach me to snowboard, so I decided that was something I could do for him, give the snowboard just one run, and then go live in San Francisco because he and I had talked about living there together one day, and it seemed like a good place to start over. So finally I made it all the way out to Big Sur. And it was this really perfect gorgeous day and the snow was pure white, like the snow on the first night I met him. And I stood up at the top of the mountain on Jason's snowboard looking down at all the trees I was somehow going to have to navigate my way around and I thought, I am insane, this is going to kill me, I mean, I still had never even been on a snowboard before. But I said to hell with it, and I pushed off the top of the mountain, and I know this sounds crazy, but I swear, I could feel Jason with me, holding me up the entire way down. And by the time I reached the bottom, I felt him let me go." Nina exhales. "And I let him go then, too." She presses her hand over her heart. "I went to San Francisco after that. And I've been there ever since." Nina turns toward me again. "Belly," she says. She's staring at me. "Don't think for even a second that I ever forgot about you or Mom. I thought about you guys every day and every time Max went to check up on you I asked him to . . ."

"Wait," I say. *"What?"*

Nina looks at me, like she's confused by my confusion. And then she nods. "Oh, right, I haven't told you that part yet," she shakes her head. "Max, Jason's best friend and the guy whose number you found, has been checking up on you and Mom. You'll probably recognize him when you meet him later."

I stare at her, blinking. "You had someone check up on us?"

"Every month for the last two years." She nods. "Max was surprised you didn't recognize his voice on the phone when you called him, actually."

I stop and look at Nina while I try and take all this in. "So you really didn't forget about us," I say.

Nina shakes her head. "Of course not, not even for a second. And all along, I was planning on coming back, I just wanted to make sure I waited long enough that it would be okay for everybody. It's funny, because only a couple weeks ago I started thinking that maybe it was time. And then Max called me and he told me what was going on, that you'd called him. It wasn't until later that we realized who you were with, but by then it was too late. When I finally heard you talking to Sean in that motel room, that was the most relieved I'd ever been in my entire life, but when I heard him almost . . ." Nina lets out a shaky breath. "How did you pull that off?"

"It was under the desk," I say. "I kicked it there and then tried to talk as loud as possible so you'd hear us."

"As soon as I heard you through the phone telling him that you were going to look for me on Haight Street, I got my friends to wait for you guys at Golden Gate Park since I figured you'd have to end up there."

"Did they follow us? After they told us your address? When we were walking over I had this feeling someone was behind us the entire time . . ."

"Of course." Nina nods. "They followed you up the hill and then you guys came into my apartment and then, this guy pointed a gun at me and my amazingly brave little sister tackled the shit out of him. And I guess you pretty much know the rest."

And then Nina nods and she collapses back against her seat, like someone who's been running and running for years and has just finally stopped.

I turn toward her. I have waited so long for this, for this story, for this moment, and I want to tell her I'm sorry for ever doubting her reasons for leaving, for being angry, for not trusting her, for everything that she's been through, but when our eyes meet, she just nods. And I realize I don't have to say anything at all because, in this moment, I can tell she already knows. And I know something then, too, this Nina, this person sitting next to me, is the sister I grew up with, the sister I love and have missed so very much, but she's not quite the same person she was when she left.

Then again, neither am I.

"Hey, Belly," Nina says. "I still want to hear *your* whole story, too. I mean, there's a whole lot of what happened that I still don't understand." And then she stops and smiles. "But I guess there'll be plenty of time for everything later."

"Plenty of time now," I say. And I smile, too.

Then Nina goes back to her drawing, and I go back to staring out the window. We'll be home soon.

# FORTY-FOUR

I see her before she sees us, my mom, standing by the baggage claim, two bouquets of yellow flowers clutched in her hands.

Nina spots her a second after I do. And then she takes off running like crazy.

"Mom!" she shouts. "MOM! MOM! MOOOOOOM!"

Our mom turns when she hears Nina's voice and then her entire face lights up. And she stands there beaming in this light blue sleeveless dress and makeup and the little gold earrings Nina and I got her for Mother's Day like ten years ago.

When Nina reaches her they throw their arms around each other, and there's hugging and crying and laughing and when I get there I get roped in to the hug, too.

Finally, after a very long time, we let go and pull back. Nina's eyes are twinkling, like they always used to. And my mother looks so happy and soft and pleased and proud, it's like the drawing of her on Nina's wall is a portrait of her from this very moment. And then she glances down at her hands like she just realized she's still holding on to the bouquets of yellow flowers, which have now been completely crushed by the fury of our hugs. She thrusts them out toward us. The remaining petals flutter to the floor.

"You're both grounded," she says. And the three of us burst out laughing.

# FORTY-FIVE

A week ago at this time is when it all began. I had just left Mon Coeur with a bag of broken cookies in my hand, and was about ten minutes away from finding Nina's drawing, and about four hours away from going to a party at the Mothership, and about seven hours away from leaning against a wall and meeting what I thought was just a friendly stranger in a mask. A week ago at this time, I could not have even begun to imagine all of the insane things that were about to happen. But now, sitting out here on lawn chairs on the sidewalk in front of Mon Coeur, I know that even if I could, I wouldn't change a single moment of the last week. Because if it had somehow gone differently, things might not be exactly the way they are right now.

"Shouldn't be too much longer," Brad says. "The fireworks usually start ten minutes after sunset."

"*You* usually start ten minutes after sunset." Thomas leans his head on Brad's shoulder.

Brad puts his arm around Thomas and pulls him in close. "I have no idea what that means, sweetness, but you're too cute to have to make sense."

There are seven of us, stretched out on the best piece of sidewalk in all of Edgebridge, on the blue and white lawn chairs that Brad found in the back room. To my right, Brad and Thomas are adding filters to a photo. To my left, Amanda is chatting with Adam, the new guy she's been seeing, and Adam's cute best friend Cody, who smiles shyly at me whenever he catches my eye.

And right there in the middle, Nina and I are eating the last bites of our ice cream sandwiches.

Nina licks her fingers, stands up, and tosses both of our wrappers in the trash. "I hope he gets here before they start," she says. And then she twists her head around, looking at the heavy crowds of people on either side of the street.

"Who?" I say. But she doesn't hear me because she's up on her tiptoes waving her arms and yelling.

"Max!" she calls out. "Maxie!" A lanky guy with bright red hair and an earring in each ear is walking toward us through the crowd.

"Hey, Pal," he says. "Hey! Hey! Hey!" They hug and he spins her around.

"Max," Nina says. "This is . . ."

"Wait a second, I know you," Brad says suddenly. "You come into Mon Coeur! You always order something quirky . . ." He snaps his fingers, trying to remember.

"Two Earl Grey tea bags with extra room for milk!" I say suddenly.

"Girl deserves a raise," Max says, grinning at me. "Sorry I had to lie to you when you called me last week." I notice his slight

Southern accent now. "That was, uh, kind of necessary at the time."

"No problem," I say. I smile back. "Drop a couple bucks in the tip jar next time you're at Mon Coeur and we'll forget all about it."

"Wait!" Amanda says, disentangling herself from Adam's giant arms. She stands up. "You're the Southern guy, who we called from Attic! The one who used to date Deb . . ."

"Well, except there is no Deb," Max/Earl Grey says. He rocks back on his heels. "That was just some quick thinking on my part." He taps his temple.

"I am so very confused," Amanda says.

"I'll explain later," I tell her.

It's almost time now.

Couples are holding hands and leaning against each other. Friends are cuddling up to snap pictures together. And directly across the street two small girls, one older, one younger, are chasing each other in circles around their parents' legs.

I turn toward Nina. She reclines a little in her seat and something white falls out of her pocket onto the grass below. I can just barely make it out now. It's the napkin Nina was sketching on during our flight home. There I am, curly hair curling in all directions, one dimple, and a crooked smile. And there she is, wavy hair, matching dimple, big grin that takes up half her face. I begin to reach out for it, but stop myself. I think I'll leave this one here for someone else to find.

"Belly." Nina pokes me in the arm. "Look up! They're starting!"

And I tip my head back just in time to see the dark summer sky fill up with light.

# Check out these other
## POINT PAPERBACKS

## *Screenshot* by Donna Cooner

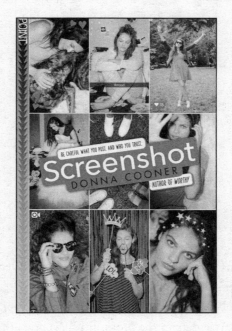

Skye's social media game is always on point. Until her best friend, Asha, films an embarrassing video of Skye at a sleepover and posts it online. Although Asha deletes the post, someone sends Skye a shocking screenshot from the video. Skye's perfect image—and privacy—are suddenly in jeopardy. What will Skye do to keep the screenshot under wraps? And who is trying to ruin her life?

# It's Not Me, It's You
## by Stephanie Kate Strohm

NATALIE WAGNER, *random freshman*: Avery Dennis—*the* Avery Dennis—got dumped right before prom.

BIZZY STANHOPE, *officially the worst*: The head of the prom committee doesn't have a date to the prom. It is beyond pathetic.

JAMES "HUTCH" HUTCHERSON, *lab partner*: Did Avery really swear off dating until she discovers why her relationships never work out? I'll believe that when I see it.

AVERY DENNIS, *recently dumped/topic of much gossip*: Okay. Everyone is talking about it, so let's talk about it . . .

# *Lucky in Love*
# by Kasie West

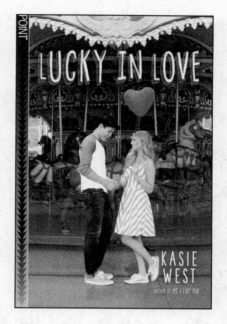

Maddie's not impulsive. She's all about hard work and planning ahead. But one night, on a whim, she buys a lottery ticket. And then, to her astonishment—she wins! In a flash, Maddie's life is unrecognizable. The only person she can trust is Seth Nguyen, her funny, charming coworker at the local zoo, who doesn't seem to know about Maddie's big news. But what will happen if he learns her secret?

# POINT PAPERBACKS
## THIS IS YOUR LIFE IN FICTION

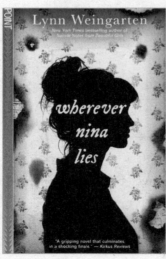

## BOOKS ABOUT LIFE. BOOKS ABOUT LOVE.
## BOOKS ABOUT YOU.

**IreadYA.com**

POINT